Brenton Udor

Short Stories

This is a work of fiction. Any references to historical events; to real people, living or dead; or real locales are intended only to give the fiction a setting in historical reality.

Other names, characters and incidents either are the product of the author's imagination or are used fictitiously, and their resemblance, if any, to real-life counterparts is entirely coincidental.

ISBN-13:978-1482016093

ISBN-10:1482016095

udor.brenton@gmail.com

Other Books by Brenton Udor

The Shawn McCormick Detective Mystery Series

The Book

Khufu's Tablet

Wrath of the Dark Circle

The Serpent's Tears

Special thanks to Tammy Christie for her tireless effort and patience

~Contents~

"For civilization to survive, the human race has to remain civilized"

Rod Serling

Short Stories

Man in a Desert

It never occurred to me that it would end like this … the dying, that is.

I'd always imagined it would be different, especially for someone like me … but this? This was almost pleasurable, 'a sigh of relief' if you will. It was as if I had been holding my breath my whole life, waiting for this moment in time.

I turned over on my side to view my surroundings. "Yep," I said in a dry-rasp, "it's still the desert alright." I chuckled at my own 'dry humor' (pardon the pun, I thought) then I chuckled more, causing me to break into a cough that racked my whole body with a quivering spasm. Now there *was* pain … and blood, blood in the sand next to me. I could see little rivulets of red running out of the gaping wound in my side and then disappearing into the parched earth that was eager to drink it up. I coughed more as I made the effort to grope into a coat pocket for the rag I had been using as a handkerchief. After finding the dirty thing, I stuffed it under my vest, over the wound. I pushed gently at first, then harder in an attempt to staunch the flow.

"How come I'm not dead yet?" I wondered out loud, craning my neck to see if I could locate my mount. I pulled my knees up as best I could, then, after considerable effort, rolled up onto them. I yelled out in pain, my voice echoing off the mesa walls that seemed to surround the few hundred acres or so of desert I had been deposited into. I took a couple of deep breaths and straightened up, still clutching the rag firmly against my left ribcage.

I had no idea how long I had been unconscious, what day it was, or mostly, who *I* was, and how I had gotten out here. My eyes found it hard to focus due to the blazing sun overhead along with the newly discovered headache that crept up behind both ears and boomed across my forehead like a Fourth of July marching band .... And now something else...

My stomach imploded, making me bend in half and gag, but nothing came out, just air.

"Oh great," I cursed, wiping my mouth with the back of a hand, "I'm gonna starve to death before I die of lead poisonin'."

I laughed like an idiot at my hopeless situation. Then I heard 'em ... gun shots ... several echoing concussions in quick succession, followed by several more. I sat up as straight as I could and closed my eyes, not only because of the sun and the pain, but in order to locate what direction the shootin' was comin' from. Try as I might, though, it was impossible to determine with this landscape. I was in a bowl surrounded by cliffs and twisting canyons. I took a deep breath and struggled to my feet. My legs wobbled as if they had a mind of their own. I staggered backward and clutched my wounded side.

I heard more *pops* and they seemed to be getting closer. I blinked, rubbed a dirty hand over my face and tried to focus. Then I saw it ... my pistol lying on the ground a few feet away. I concentrated on the gun, then took as many steps as my body would allow to get to it. I collapsed back down on my knees before it. I shook my head to clear the stars that seem to come outta nowhere and spin around my eye sockets. I blinked several times more, focused on the weapon and reached down.

"There you are ... how'd ya get over here?" I asked, as I shook the sand out of the barrel. I ran the back of my coat sleeve across my now sweaty forehead. Then I checked the chambers to see if the thing was loaded. It was a six-shooter, my granddaddy's. "Well, what'da ya know, at least I remembered that," I thought in surprise. Two chambers held empty cartridges, the rest were live. I heard more shots now, booming over my shoulder to my left, then to my right ... all around me, from everywhere it seemed, echoing like thunder.

"Well, partner," I said, speaking to the gun as I wiped it off the best I could, "you shot twice at somethin' fer sure ... I'll be dipped if I can remember what though. Now the question is, do I fire you off and see who's doin' the shoot'n out here and maybe they come and finish off my sorry hide, or do I sit here and die of my wound and exposure?"

I cocked the hammer back and forth several times to free up the action and then it occurred to me …if that was a huntin' party out there, I might as well stick the barrel into my big mouth and pull the trigger one last time ….

I looked around and sighed. "Decisions, decisions," I muttered to myself, then laughed out loud. "Well, guess we'll see who's out there. I'll make sure to save one for myself, just in case."

I cocked the hammer back, raised the weapon over my head and pulled the trigger. The shot rang out, the sound of it bouncing off every cliff that surrounded me, echoing and re-echoing until there was silence. I rested the gun in my lap, sat back on my haunches and waited for what seemed like forever. Then, suddenly, more repeats, but now louder and closer than before.

"Well, looks like somebody's interested," I said and then raised the weapon again, firing off another round. "Two dogs left," I whispered, "better save 'em for whoever's comin, or …"

I stood back up, wobbled, and planted my feet firmly. I pushed the now almost soaked rag against my ribcage with my left hand and held the pistol in my right. I could feel myself getting weaker by the second as the rag became more and more saturated with my blood. Maybe whoever was comin' closer had better shake a leg or they would find me unconscious and easy pickins.

Finally, I could make out dots on the horizon. Most likely comin' from one of the canyon openings to this isolated little valley. The heat rising off the desert floor made the approaching dots swirl and dance before my eyes. I blinked against the unmerciful star overhead, repeatedly wiping my face with my sleeve as best I could with my gun hand. More shots rang out from the approaching dots as they bounced towards me and I braced myself for the whiz of bullets I expected to strike. But, to my surprise, that didn't happen.

I raised my weapon at the nearest dot, cocked back the hammer and waited while what little sweat I had left in my weakening body ran down my face and neck. There seemed to be a dozen or so riders bearing down on me and, just for an instant, I thought I saw the flicker of ... feathers ... feathers and long hair.

I sighed and closed my eyes against the scalding sunlight, licking my dry lips. I laughed one last time as I raised the pistol and placed the end of the barrel against my right temple. I felt the cocked hammer against my thumb ....

"Send me home partner," I said to the gun.

It never occurred to me that it would end like this ... the dying, that is. It was almost pleasurable ... 'a sigh of relief' if you will. It was as if I had been holding my breath my whole life, waiting for this moment in time. I felt myself falling … falling backward into oblivion … falling until …

I came to just long enough to see dry desert ground moving quickly under and past me … oh, and there were legs. My arms were stretched out, dangling in front of me and were knocking against the hairy legs of whatever kinda beast I had been thrown over as it bumped and galloped over the rough ground.

“Maybe,” I remember thinkin’, “this was some kind of supernatural way I was being transported to hell … on the back of some demonic monster.”

The vision, if that’s what it was, didn’t last long, as blackness engulfed me again … the kinda darkness I imagined I would never wake up from.

~2~

When I did reopen my eyes, I found myself lying outstretched, cleaned up and naked in a transparent tub of what felt like warm goo. As I looked up I was surrounded by blue skies with little wisps of clouds floating by … and by a strange, low, humming sound that seemed to radiate from underneath me. Then a face appeared in my line of vision … a woman's face, soft and beautiful, with close cropped black hair and deep brown eyes. I tried to speak, but nothin' came out but a grunt due to some sort of a breathing gizmo hooked to a hose that had been inserted into my mouth and partway down my throat. The woman deftly removed the bit, causing a small column of white mist to escape. She smiled down at me and then inserted another, much smaller, tube between my lips. She seemed to mouth "Drink" without sayin' a word. The liquid was cool and refreshing and I drank until I was satisfied. She smiled down at me again, nodded and then turned away briefly.

“Am I in heaven? Are you an angel?” I heard my voice ask.

Then I heard her speak. “He’s awake, Doctor.”

The beautiful woman was replaced by a concerned man’s face lookin’ down at me. He began methodically pulling up both my eyelids and shining a very bright light into each eye ... the light seemed to be coming from the tip of his finger!

“He’s stable for now,” he said, speaking to someone, probably her. “Tell the pilot to make his best speed for the hospital. Have him tell traffic control that we need a free corridor of uncluttered airspace to the E.R. Inform the medical staff that we have a male, early fifties, with a lead projectile wound, lower left side. Tell them he’s dehydrated, sun burnt, disoriented and has been overexposed to Ground-Rads ... I’ve stabilized with suspension-gel, cleared the lungs with Bio-mist and have given a 10cc dermal infusion of NANO-mites to counteract infection”.

“Yes, Doctor, right away,” a kindly female voice replied.

“Where am I?” I rasped, my head beginning to swim.

“Just take it easy, Marshal,” the man replied, placing a hand on my shoulder. “You’re in a MediVAC Transport Skimmer on our way to SouthDOME, New Colorado. Do you remember what happened to you?”

My mouth opened and closed like a gold fish suckin’ air.

"Uh, no. I'm guessin' I got shot .... By the way, am I dead?"

The doctor smiled. "Not on my watch."

Well, long story short, I woke up again sometime later, yawned, scratched my rump and attempted to get outta the bed I was in. That didn't happen as my head came into contact with something invisible that seemed to disagree with what I was tryin' to do and gently pushed me back down.

"Stasis Field," I muttered. Then I smiled as I realized my memory was comin' back ... well, pieces of it. A few minutes later, I heard a soft tone in the room and the sound of a door *whoosh* to the side to allow a white clad MedTech to enter. She was as pretty as the one on the skimmer, but foreign lookin', at least to me. She came over to the bed and smiled down at me. She was tall and lean, short haired, with an odd reddish tint to it. What stood out to me, though, was her eyes ... they were amber in color and large in her head without being out of proportion. She reached into a pocket of her uniform, which was more of a body-suit, and retrieved a small square card which she ran her thumb over. This caused the stasis field above me to snap off and to reveal her to me even more clearly... especially those large eyes.

"How are you feeling today, Marshal?" she asked brightly, with a slight accent I knew I had heard before, but for the life of me couldn't place.

"Well, darlin', I'm as good as I'm gonna be for now, seein' as how I prolly should be dead," I replied hoarsely.

“Yes, you did give everyone a fright,” she said in agreement. “But now let me check your vitals before we talk about some specifics, alright?”

“Fine with me, darlin’,” I said, smilin’ wolfishly back.

She returned the smile and nodded, then proceeded to remove a portable object off the side of the bed and enter, on a touch screen, several commands. Instantly, a variety of multicolored beams of light emanated from a panel in the ceiling above me, passing, like strips, over and over my body which was clothed in white, gauze-like fabric. While this ‘light-show’ was goin’ on, she studied the readouts on her screen, nodded several times and then replaced it, magnetically, onto the side of my bed.

“Well now,” she replied, making a few notes on another device she removed from a pocket, “you seem fit enough to be allowed a bit of recreation. How does that sound?” she asked.

I just smiled and winked up at her. I thought for a moment I saw her face turn slightly pink but maybe I imagined it. She looked away, briefly, pursed her lips and shook her head.

“I was warned about you, Marshal,” she said in a mock-scold, as she crossed her arms over her chest. Then she smiled warmly. “I guess you *are* feeling better ... and what I meant was, you will be allowed to get around a bit in a hover-chair, but only within the limits of the facility, to and from your therapy and rehabilitation sessions and, if you're good, to the observation decks. Nothing outside in the atmosphere for the time being, understand?"

"Huh? What therapy? Rehab? Look, darlin', I gave up drinkin' years ago and besides ..."

She held up one long index finger and cleared her throat, "First of all, *Cowboy*, I believe that's what they used to call your ancestors, it's Doctor ... Doctor Xihn. Second, you have been severely wounded. That metal projectile you were struck with caused considerable soft tissue and muscle damage to your lower left quadrant, you've lost considerable blood, body fluids, a rib, *and* we barely managed to save your kidney. We prefer trying to regrow the damaged area rather than give you an artificial organ. Then there's the damage to your lungs due to your prolonged exposure to the naturally occurring Zeta Radiation in the area you were found in. By the way, what were you thinking ... being out there alone without a proper respirator? Not even a *Noob* would be so foolish, I must say ..."

She went on for a few more sentences until she caught herself and apologized for her abruptness.

"At any rate, your lungs are being rebuilt as we speak. We've given you enough NANO-mites and tissue infusions that hopefully will do the job, but it's going to take time, understand? So, 'no riding off into the sunset' according to the novels I understand you enjoy reading."

"Uh, yes, ma'am, I understand ... sorry for the trouble," I sheepishly replied.

"No trouble, Marshal, that's why we're here," she said with a grin.

"Oh, uh, by the way ... is my name 'Marshal'?"

The doctor's eyes grew even wider now.

"Why, no ... you *are* a Marshal, that is, a Law Enforcement Officer stationed somewhere on the Southern Rim, don't you remember?"

I rubbed my face with both hands. "Doc, I barely remember anythin' that happened out there. What's that about?"

"It's probably due to the trauma you've experienced and the radiation exposure. We hoped your disorientation when you arrived would leave but apparently we need to run some neural scans and make an evaluation. I will schedule this at once ..." she said as she, again, fingered a device.

"So I've lost-a few 'marbles,' huh?" I asked.

"Marbles?" the doctor replied curiously, her forehead wrinkling.

"Yeah, you know, marbles ... little round glass balls kids play with?"

The doctor just stood there, bit her bottom lip, and slowly shook her head.

"Do ya mean to tell me you never heard of a marble?" I asked skeptically, "where're you from anyway?"

"Why, right here. I'm a native," she replied.

“I thought you looked injun,” I said.

“Injun’?” she repeated. “I’m sorry, Marshal, but I’m not ‘Injun’ ... in fact, I’m not familiar with that designation. I’m *Menutan*, a native of this world. Do you know where you are?”

I began to rub my face again with a mix of confusion and sudden exhaustion.

“Alright, enough for now ... sleep,” she said, snapping the stasis field back on.

“Oh, now look, Doc, I don’t need that, I ...”

“We don’t want you falling out of bed or doing something ‘Cowboy-ish’, now do we, Marshal, hmm?” she replied firmly. “Besides, I’ve been informed that you have guests on their way to visit you. They’re traveling some distance, so let’s get you rested and tested so I can give them an intelligent diagnosis and *you* can give them an intelligent report when they arrive.”

“Sounds like I’m in some kinda trouble,” I replied.

Doctor Xhin smiled crookedly. “That would not surprise me. Now sleep.”

It was later the following day that my visitors arrived just as that native Doctor *Zie-een*, or whatever her name was, had said. I waited for ‘em in one of the observation lounges that jutted out from the side of the hospital facility and overlooked the city. I had gotten myself there under my own steam in a hover chair that scooted on a cushion of magnetic flux .... At least that’s how it was explained to me after some pretty odd looks. I should have known this, I guess, at least according to the Neuro-Psycho Trauma expert I spoke with earlier. He claimed that I was sufferin' from a form of amnesia. I could remember some things, kinda, but not others, like who *I* was. I couldn't remember my name fer cryin' out loud! (I asked several times about that, but seems like everybody got real dumb all of a sudden when I did and that made me plumb sore.) I also asked about what happened in that hell-hole of a desert, and how I got shot and by who ... and basically this whole world I was on. The psych doctor, at one point, asked me where I thought I was ...

"Well partner," I replied, "I gotta feelin' this ain't Earth."

"Earth? You mean Terra, our home world?" the doctor asked.

"Uh, okay ... I seem to remember it just being called planet Earth ... change the name did they?"

The doctor pulled on his ear lobe several times before he answered.

"Yes, some time ago, I'm afraid."

"How long ago?"

He cleared his throat. "Several centuries. Look, Marshal, you've suffered some trauma and it's just going to take some time to sort out ...."

"Oh fer cryin' out loud in a barn!" I barked, "save the psyco-babble! I know who I am ... uh, 'cept for my name ... but I know my roots, ya hear?"

"And what are they?"

"Well, best I can recall, my kin comes from Cochise County, State of Arizona, United States of America, planet Earth, by golly!"

The hover chair commenced to jumpin' some under me the more excited I got.

"Whoa there partner," I said to the thing, "don't be buckin' me off just yet."

"Just relax, Marshal, the device will respond to your reflexes, just move naturally," the doctor cautioned. "So," he continued, "you feel you weren't born here then?"

I wrung my face in one hand and sighed heavily. "Look, I dunno. By the way, where's *here* anyway?"

The doc looked at me for a few long moments before answering.

"Well, *here* is the Proxima Centauri Star System. We are on the third planet called Terra Mynos1. It's approximately three times the mass of, well, Earth ... if I remember my historical geography correctly.

I cleared my throat, not knowing really how to respond as I tried to make sense out of it.

"Uh, how far away is that from home, I mean Earth?" I asked.

"About four light years I believe."

"What the blazes is a 'light year?'"

“Look, Marshal ...”

“I know, never mind ... okay, answer me this, Doc, what’s a ‘My-noo-tan’?

“It’s pronounced ‘*Menutan*’ and they are the original inhabitants of this world. They’re humanoid, peaceful and highly intelligent.”

“Like that doctor I’ve met ... what’s her name again?”

“Xihn; and there are others.”

“I’m sorry; I can’t wrap my tongue around that handle. I’m just gonna call her Sue or Sally or ...”

“Just ‘Doctor’ will be fine, I’m sure. Look, your memory will return in time and in pieces. Just be patient with the healing process.”

“I’m already a ‘patient’ gul-darn it! I just, well ...”

“What? Tell me.”

“I just don’t feel like I belong in this, *on this* planet, this century, this place fer Pete’s sake!” I said angrily.

“Well, Marshal, I’m afraid you’re stuck. It’s a very long walk back to Earth.”

And, so I sat in my floatin’ chair in a plastic room lookin’ out on a cityscape that was artificially grown inside a plastic dome. I sat there watchin’ lines of traffic crawl through the air like swarms of insects.

“I’m part of this mess?” I kept askin’ myself in disbelief. Some of it was vaguely familiar, like I dreamt it once or read it in a book. Other aspects of it was just plain strange, unreal, and it made me uneasy and wanna be straddling a horse somewhere out on the prairie ... and I mean a *real* horse, like back on Earth ... the four legged kind. Not like the weird critter I was slung over like a piece of old carpet. What'd somebody say they were called, *Mugwahts* or some such nonsense? Reminded me (what little I remembered of the ride) of a cross between a buffalo, a Gila-lizard, and a nightmare. I sat there ponderin' about that critter, along with the last few days, my wounds, the tests, and what I've been told and *not* been told. I was about ready to shoot something (if I had my pistol) when I heard the door slide open behind me. I turned my body and the chair moved with me.

There in the doorway stood three people, a young woman and two men. One of the men was around my age, maybe a little younger, a big fella, dressed in some kinda uniform with a badge or a patch pasted on the front of his shirt, just above where a pocket should be. The other man was older, dressed in a business suit of a sort I wasn't familiar with. I didn't recognize either of 'em. Now the young woman, on the other hand ....

"I know you ... I think ..." I blurted out loud and pointing my finger at her.

"Yeah, daddy, it's me!" she replied, with tears now running down her face. She covered the distance between her and me at a fast gallop. When she was close enough she threw her arms around my neck and practically hugged the life outta me.

“Easy there, girl, I’m wounded,” I said into her ear.

“Oh, daddy, we were so worried,” she said, pulling away and looking me over.

“I’m fine girl … but look, I’m havin’ a little trouble figurin’ out just what happened. First things first though: You say you’re my kid? What’s yer name?”

She stood back and blinked with surprise. “They told us your eggs got scrambled, but …”

“No buts, who are ya?” I asked again, taking hold of her shoulders.

“You really don’t remember?” one of the men responded.

“No! Now stand there and shut up!” I barked. “Alright, girl, answer my question straight. What’s yer name?”

“My name is Josie … Josie Earp.”

“And what’s *my* name?”

She swallowed hard before she answered.

“Your name is Wyatt … you’re Wyatt Earp.”

I let loose of her shoulders and sat back. ‘Wyatt Earp,’ that name sounded familiar … historical … that was *my* name? I felt a headache comin’ on and I tried to rub it outta my forehead.

“Boss, you okay?” the uniformed man asked.

“Boss? I’m yer boss? Who are ya?” I asked, looking

up at him.

They all took turns staring at each other then back at me. The big fella cleared his throat.

"I'm your deputy, Sam Holland. C'mon Wyatt, ya gotta remember."

I looked at him long and hard … nothin'.

"Sorry, Sam, you don't ring any bells," I replied.

Sam put both hands on his hips, cursed and shook his head.

"Now what're we supposed to do, huh?" he griped.

"Never mind, Sam," the other fella said. "Wyatt, how about me, do you know me?"

I stared at him too but still drew deuces. "Sorry, mister. Who are ya?" I asked.

The man in the suit sighed heavily. "I'm your family lawyer and friend, Mathew Fletcher … and you're in trouble, Marshal."

"Oh not now, Matt," Josie sighed back.

"Trouble? What kinda trouble?" I asked.

"Look, daddy, you do all you can do to get yourself well. You never mind about anything else. We're here to help … and take you home."

"Josie, you know that's not a good idea right now the way things are back there," Sam replied.

"Alright, everybody just shut up and tell me what's

goin' on?" I snapped.

"Well now, how're we supposed to do that if ya just told us to shut up?" Sam replied loudly.

"Sam," Josie said, looking crossly over at him.

"Yeah, yeah ..." he said, turning and walkin' away. "His disposition hasn't changed much," he muttered, as he stood by the transparent wall and looked out on the city.

"What's his problem?" I said, pointing with my thumb at him.

"Folks, why don't we all just sit down and talk everything through, alright?" Matt suggested.

"Suits me," I said. I maneuvered my little vehicle across the room to where there was a table and a few chairs. Josie went over, pulled on Sam's arm and whispered something. The deputy reluctantly complied, followed her over to the others, and sat down heavily into one of the chairs. Everyone made themselves comfortable, but said nothing for a few long minutes.

"Alright, look folks," I finally said, scratching the stubble on my face, "I'm stuck here, shot up and stupid. Just somebody start from the beginnin' and tell me more about who I am and what happened to me out there."

I pointed my thumb back toward the great outdoors (or indoors, seein' as how the whole town was stuck in a fish bowl).

“Alright daddy, just sit there and listen, okay? I’ll start,” Josie replied.

She pinched the area between her eyes momentarily, took a deep breath and began.

“Your name is Wyatt Lewis Earp and you live here on Mynos with me, Sam, Billy, who’s another deputy who couldn’t come, and Jake, the cook. We all share quarters at the SouthRIM District Law Enforcement Office Complex, South West Territory. You’re the Regional Security Director or ‘Marshal’, appointed by the Home Office at Adelaide, the Capital City at NorthDome. That’s where the first human colony was established on this world about a century and a half ago. You probably don’t remember much history ... fact is, most of the time you don’t give a good hoot about local history, but just in case you care now, here goes.

“When we, that is, when the first colonists landed here, the natives, the *Menutan*, were in pretty tough shape, dying out actually .... some dormant genetic mutation, along with the planets magnetic field shifting ... somethin’ like that ... I’m not a scientist, so I don’t claim to understand it, but, apparently, our people did. So we worked together, showed them how to make habitation domes from the sand and environmental suits to block out the radiation coming from the planet’s core. The radiation is not so bad here or in other places, depending on the latitude, but where they found you, in that desert, the Rads were pretty intense without protective gear ....” She lost her temper and stood. “Which you *didn’t* wear, in fact, you *never* wear, of all the stubborn, knot-headed, stupid things to do! How many times did ..."

She raved on for a few minutes, wagging a finger at me and using language I've never heard. Mathew, the lawyer, urged her to calm down. Sam reached over and gave her what looked like a stick of chewin' gum. She calmed down, put the gum in her mouth, and stood there chewing furiously.

"Hang on a second, uh, Josie," I said, interrupting and slightly overwhelmed by her outburst, "how old are you anyhow?"

"I'm twenty-three."

"Where's your momma?"

Everyone looked down or away momentarily. Then Josie, still chewing furiously, answered. "She died when I was ten! And, that's when *your* life went to hell in a hand basket lemme tell ya ..."

"Alright, Josie, take it easy!" Sam protested, reaching across the table and taking her arm.

"Oh, I'm fine, lemme go," she replied, snatching her arm away.

"Josie, simmer down," Mathew added, "your daddy doesn't have a clue ... remember what the doctor told us."

She scowled, seemed to getta-hold of herself and then plopped back down. "Yeah, yeah ... sorry ... sorry, daddy," she apologized.

I had the overwhelming urge to scoop her up into my arms, but I didn't. I just sat there and stared, hoping soon I was gonna wake up from all this and be home in my bed. I cleared my throat several times to remove the lump.

"How?" I managed to get out.

Josie rubbed the back of her neck. "She got sick and died," she replied simply.

"With the kinda doctors I've seen around here?" I said skeptically, and looking straight at her.

"Josie," Sam said quietly, "best tell 'em the truth."

Josie looked over at him, then at the ceiling, after that she ran her tongue across her mouth and spoke.

"She died of gunshot wounds after a surprise raid on the compound," she said grimly.

"Raid? What raid? I thought them *Menutan* folk were friendly?" I said.

"*They* are, but not the ... (language I was surprised to hear come outta a young woman's mouth) ... renegades who land here from time to time," Josie angrily spat.

"Renegades?" I responded.

"Off world marauders, outlaws ... pirates, if you will. They attack and rob the outlying settlements, mining operations and off world shipping lanes," Mathew added.

“Pirates?” I replied, scratching my head with disbelief.

“That’s right, Wyatt ... like them savage injuns you read about in them old books you always got your face stuck in,” Sam added.

“And those journals you got on file in the archives about your great, great granddaddy back on Earth, remember? You’re named after him,” Josie said.

I looked at the three of ‘em tryin’ to remember some tidbit of what they were talkin’ about, but I was still in a fog.

“So yer sayin’ your mother, my wife, was murdered?” I said.

“Yes,” all three replied.

I felt my face turn bright red. “Did ya get ‘em?”

They all commenced looking at each other again.

“Well?” I pressed.

“Yeah, one or two,” Sam said, “but not their leader. He’s the one who ...” Something caught in his throat.

“He’s the one who killed momma. A man called Judas Long,” Josie finished for him.

“Wyatt, he’s the one you were after in the Badlands. The area where the search party found you. Apparently you were ambushed and left for dead,” Mathew said.

“Wyatt, you got yourself bushwhacked like a greenhorn out there ‘cuz you’re too pig-headed to wait for a proper posse!” Sam barked, slapping an open hand on the table top.

Everyone lowered their eyes and said nothing.

“Well,” I began after awhile, “I wanna say I’m sorry for the trouble I’ve caused. Sounds to me like I’m a real pain in the ...”

“Daddy, it’s alright, nobody’s faulting ya,” Josie cut in.

“No, no, girl, I need to either get my mind back or relearn some things, looks like. Maybe it’s a good thing I don’t remember some of this, I dunno ....” I stopped and turned the chair to face the outside world. “This all seems like a bad dream to me ... all that out there,” I pointed out to the panorama of the busy city, “I don’t see how I fit into all this.”

“You don’t,” Josie replied. “You and momma never did. It’s like you two shoulda been born in another time and place.”

“Yeah, the old Earth West, far as I could ever tell,” Sam added.

“Fact is, Wyatt, you’re a natural born lawman, just like your father and his father when they migrated. The Planetary Commission that governs things around here appreciates all that the Earps have done to try to civilize this world over the years... and it ain’t been easy,” Mathew stated.

"Ain't there no military here?" I asked, turning back around and trying to sit up straighter.

They all smirked. "Wyatt, after a century or so, the human population here is barely hanging on," Mathew replied.

"Huh?" I said, "what's all that out there?" I pointed behind me.

"Oh that?" Mathew continued, "That isn't what it looks like, all that air traffic zooming by. Most of it is robotic...automated for our convenience. Shows how intelligent we are, I guess. Oh, we can build fancy machines and cities out of the sand, but we can't seem to find a way to reproduce our own kind out here, that's the real and current problem."

"But I don't get it," I replied. "This ain't the only city on this rock, right? I mean look at it," I exclaimed. "I'd swear there's over a hundred thousand folks living out there ...."

"There used to be daddy," Josie said, "in all the DOMEs across the planet. There used to be millions of us, but something happened over time. I dunno what."

"Some kinda sickness I heard," Sam replied.

"Well, the Genetic Doctors say the problem is with us. Us humans trying to adapt to an alien environment, a different star over our heads, the unusual radiation coming from the ground, in the air .... Fact is, it killed many of the first colonists when they landed. Then, after a while, we seemed to adapt, at least in these latitudes. Then we found a way to help the *Menutans* and ourselves survive here. Look, I don't claim to understand it either. I'm a lawyer basically without a practice these days. All I know is that, for a time we flourished, then over the last generation or so the birth rate has plummeted so that now days very few are able to have children and we need to pile more and more of the everyday work onto what we call BoTs ... mechanical devices."

"Fancy machines?" I replied. They all nodded.

"Well, they've been hell-bent on tryin' to mix us up with the natives," Sam said, shaking his head slowly.

"Huh?" I grunted.

"Daddy, what Sam means is that some folks are trying to mate with the *Menutan* race in an effort to preserve our species on this world. The doctors are working on it, I guess."

"And has it worked?" I asked.

"From what I understand, in some cases, yes," Mathew replied. "The children seem hardier and more adapted to the environment, like the natives here ... but it's not a perfect science yet, if I can call it that."

I rubbed my face and chuckled. "I gotta be dreamin' this," I said out loud. "So, does the planet have a large injun population?"

"Actually no," Mathew said. "Their species doesn't reproduce as often as ours does ... that's one of the problems with our mating with them. From what I understand their gestation period takes years. Rather unfortunate for us."

"I don't like it," Sam said. "It ain't natural."

"And *our* slowly dying off as a race is?" Josie replied back to him.

"This is a very controversial and heated subject in some circles," Mathew said soberly.

"I can see that," I said. "Reminds me of how the settlers felt about the injuns' in the Old West."

"You mean what you read about the 'Old West'?" Sam corrected.

"Well ... okay, I guess I musta read it ... sure feels like I lived it though."

Josie cleared her throat. "After momma died ... and the funeral, you just got lost in them old books and your ancestry," she said. "You'd be gone for days, sometimes weeks out there beyond the Rim, out in the badlands. We thought for a while you were never gonna come home. But then, after a time, you seemed to snap outta it, and get back to your duties as Marshal, but you were never really the same."

"I'll say, especially when you got reports of possible sightings of them renegades landing somewhere out there. You were on a mount and gone before the rest of us knew what was goin' on," Sam complained.

"Really," I commented. "So, these renegades, what're they like?"

"Oh, they're 'human' enough," Sam replied, "bunch'a no account descendants of convicts that escaped custody years ago, or so we've been told."

“Yes, in a manner of speaking,” Mathew continued. “According to the history, the ARK transports that originally got us here spent years in space. At some point, for whatever reason, there was a mutiny on board one of the ships. A few even died, but it was suppressed and the violators were locked up until we arrived in this star system. Well, amidst the hubbub of everything, they escaped and lit out on their own in some of the smaller intersolar ships. We never had the time or the manpower to go after them. We had all we could do to survive on this world. After a time, we just assumed they had all died out there in space somewhere, but apparently they didn’t and from time to time they return from wherever their base is to scavenge supplies, parts, technology, basically whatever they can lay their hands on.”

“That’s right. They seem to favor the extreme outpost compounds and smaller settlements near the Southern and Northern Rims. They don’t have the weapons to attack any of the major DOMEs,” Sam added.

“Thank God,” Josie sighed. “That’s all we need.”

“So, no fancy weapons with all this science we got flyin’ around?” I asked.

“Oh, you mean energy weapons?” Mathew asked.

“Yeah, I guess so … seems like I recall readin’ somethin’ about that kinda stuff,” I said.

“Oh, we have energy weapons,” Mathew said.

“They just won’t work here,” Sam added.

"Why not?"

"The magnetic field and the natural radiation neutralizes that kind of technology to the point that, well, you can probably give yourself a rash or sunburn with one, but nothing lethal."

"So, how do ya defend yourselves?"

"We've made weapons ... like your Colt," Sam replied. "They fire a projectile from a cartridge with a chemically based propellant. Here, I have one in my pocket."

Sam rummaged around in a slit in his uniform and removed a black, bullet looking object and placed it on the table.

"Guns aren't allowed in the city DOMEs, no need for 'em, so I can't show you the weapon this fits into," he said.

I picked it up, examined it, and handed it back.

"They sure don't look like much," I said.

"Well, they'll put a hole in ya," Sam chuckled. "And ya won't even know you've been shot."

"How's that?"

"No noise," Sam replied. "Not like them old powder based guns."

"Wait a minute; I heard gunfire ... a lot of gunfire, like thunder, out there on that desert. That's what got my attention and why I fired back," I replied.

Josie smiled. "Those weren't these standard issue colonial weapons. No, sir, those were 'Earp Specials', your redesign, daddy!"

"Yep, the ammo made with real gunpowder too," Sam laughed. "You had 'em issued to all law enforcement that worked under you over the years."

"The Colt Model 1873 'Peacemaker,' like my great granddaddy's...." I muttered.

Josie smiled widely and grabbed my arm. "Daddy, you remember?"

"I guess I remember that," I smiled back. "It was the weapon that won the West back on Earth in them days, no reason not to resurrect it to keep the peace in this place."

"Those were your father's words exactly to the Public Safety Commission when he brought up the idea of arming some of the deputies when he was Marshal," Mathew replied. "A few were replicated, along with a limited supply of powder-based ammunition, but it was you, when you took over his job as a young man, that polished up the design and pushed for more of them to be standard issue, at least in your jurisdiction. Of course, as time went on, there was less and less need for Law Enforcement, among the human population anyway. Then those renegades started showing up more often and ..."

"My father was Marshal here?" I interrupted.

"Yes," Josie answered. "Grandpa was a good man.

Fact is, he and Sam's daddy worked together for years."

"I hate to ask ... what happened to him?"

"Nothing bad, just old age, both of 'em," Mathew replied. "You two boys were all the family they had ... and now Josie here," he said, winking at her.

I smiled over at her. Then ..."How 'bout you Sam, got any kids?" I asked.

"Nope, not yet, but me and the misses are tryin' sure enough ... but it's like we were talkin' about earlier, it's tough to make babies on this rock."

I now changed the subject. "You folks said when you first walked in here that I was in some kinda trouble. Let's hear about it."

More awkward silence followed.

"Well, Wyatt, you went and did what you usually do when someone calls in and claims to have sighted a renegade landing," Sam finally said.

"And what's that?"

"Grab your gear, a vehicle, or a mount, and head out there *alone.*"

"And I do this because?"

"Because you feel that you're the right hand of God when it comes to momma's killer," Josie replied with irritation, "and that the rest of us need to just keep our mouths shut, stay in our place and do our jobs while you go hunting through a million square miles of desert and wasteland on a hunch that maybe you'll run into the same gang that hit our compound years ago."

"The problem, Marshal, is that this time you were formally warned by the Law Enforcement Commission, that we all work for, *not* to go after them renegades, period, until further notice as it would hinder the negotiations," Mathew added.

"Negotiations?" I repeated in surprise.

"Yes, that's right," Mathew continued, "the Colonial Government has been trying to negotiate a truce with the renegades in order to spare any more loss of life or materials in light of the dwindling population, no doubt on both sides. Your personal war with them is not conducive to progress. However, as usual, you've ignored the order and ..."

"How many?" I asked grimly.

"Well," Sam said, "the search party followed the bodies until they found your mount, dead from exhaustion. Then they followed your trail into the 'High Risk Zone' ..."

"He means 'high radiation' daddy," Josie cut in. Sam continued.

"Then they found another body, along with your empty rifle, and tracks heading into the canyons. They started shootin' into the air hopin' they'd attract your attention, *if* you were still alive that is ... looks like they got to ya just in time, *this* time," Sam said, slowly shaking his head and smiling crookedly.

“You’re just a hard man to kill, Wyatt,” he concluded.

That statement was followed by a chorus of ‘amens’ from the other two in the room.

“So,” I began to say slowly, “did I get the son-of-a …”

“We dunno,” Sam quickly replied, “the priority was to get *you* outta there. The search parties were gonna go back for the dead later, or what was left of ‘em …”

“Huh? What’da ya mean: ‘What was ‘left of ‘em?” I replied.

“Oh, I guess you don’t remember,” Josie said, “this planet has a life form, kinda like a wolf … well, more like a jackal. They run in large packs. They’re flesh eating, carrion mostly, nasty things … we shoot ‘em a lot ‘round the compound … anyway, besides that, after they found you, the area was hit by a *Siehophee* … it’s what the natives call a sand storm …”

“It’s a magnetic storm actually,” Mathew cut in, “rather violent. We get them in this latitude from time to time, but the DOMEs protect the cities. Sometimes they last for days or weeks.”

“Yes,” Josie continued, “the point is, between the wolf packs and the sand storm, well, it don’t look promisin’ to find and bring back any bodies from down there … so we don’t know if you got *him* or not …. Sorry.”

At this point, all I could do was sigh and rub my face like it was crawlin’ with spiders.

“Daddy, you okay?” Josie asked, moving closer.

“Probably not,” I replied, confused in thought. My chest hurt inside, my side hurt outside, and I felt lost and … old … useless.

“I could use a drink,” I heard myself say.

“I got ya covered, boss,” Sam replied with a smile, quickly getting up and headin’ towards the entrance where a square, silver looking suitcase sat on the floor. He snatched it up and brought it over to the table.

“This ain’t hospital policy I’m sure, but …”

He placed a palm over a particular area of the thing and a female voice announced “permission granted” causing the case to pop open. He took out several collapsible containers that became ‘drinking glasses’ and then finally he pulled out a glass bottle of …”

“J.D. 2012,” he announced proudly, holding the ancient looking bottle up. He opened the top and poured everyone a good measure of the hearty smelling brew. “Glad ta have ya back, Wyatt!” he toasted.

The others followed suit, and we all drank. It burned all the way down. We all blinked through our tears, wheezed and tried to catch our breath … that’s when the doctor walked in.

“Do I smell distilled vegetation?” Dr. Xihn asked, her large eyes growing even larger.

“Uh, no ma’am … I mean, ya see …” Sam sputtered.

"Doctor Xihn," Mathew took over, "we were just engaging in an old Earth tradition of ..."

"Killing my patient?" she stated firmly, cutting him off. "You humans seem to have an absolute proclivity for health endangering 'traditions' despite your science to the contrary," she additionally remarked.

"Uh, sorry, Doctor," Josie said by way of a group apology, while Sam put the bottle safely away.

"So, Doc, what's the verdict?" I asked, trying not to cough.

"How do you feel?" she asked.

"Like I been rode hard and put away wet," I replied.

"And shot!" Sam chipped in.

"I'm more concerned with your lungs Mr. Earp," she replied, taking out a pocket scanner and running it over my chest.

"Well?" Josie inquired.

"Adequate ... for now, I suppose," Doctor Xhin carefully replied, replacing the scanner back into a pocket. "Now, about the other matter," she continued.

"Other matter?" I said.

"Yes, Marshal, the matter of the official looking men who are in the administrative office with a warrant to take you into custody," she replied, raising an eyebrow.

"What! What men?" Josie yelped as she stood up.

"Simmer down," Mathew cautioned, "I expected some fallout over this, but not an arrest. Where's the office, Doctor?" he asked.

She politely gave him directions and he quietly left, advising as he did so that everyone was to just relax and stay put.

"Now," the doctor said, turning to me, "I want you to place this gently between your teeth, seal your lips around it and breathe in and out slowly," she said, taking out a strange looking apparatus from another large pocket in her white smock and putting the mouthpiece next to my face.

"Uh, look, Doc, is this ..." I attempted to object.

"Open," she ordered firmly.

I opened, it went in, and then I closed and began to breathe while small puffs of mist vented out each side of the thing.

"Now," she continued, "while we're waiting, why don't you two explain to me why your people want to arrest this man?" she asked, looking over at Josie and Sam who were more than willing to take turns relating the whole story while I just sat there and breathed. About a half-hour or so later, they finished as Mathew came back into the room.

"So, what's the verdict?" Sam asked on seeing him.

"Wyatt," Mathew said, looking directly at me, "you're hamstrung pretty good, I'm afraid. They got a warrant and a couple of Security Police to take you into custody and transport you to a detection center in

Adelaide pending some kind of hearing scheduled for who knows when."

I crudely spat the breathing gizmo outta my mouth onto the table top. "And this is because I was huntin' the killers who attacked my family and threaten the peace?" I said angrily.

"Well, Wyatt, I guess it ain't that simple," Mathew replied. "They got a whole world to deal with and ..."

"Oh hogwash!" I barked, "they're politicians! They outta string 'em all up! You don't negotiate with criminals, especially if they've drawn innocent blood. You hunt 'em down and bring 'em to justice or they'll back shoot ya the first chance they get, mark my words."

"Spoken like a true nineteenth-century lawman," Mathew said quietly, "but, the problem is, this isn't 1875, and this isn't Earth ... and, quite frankly, you're not the same man your ancestor was. Now, I realize you would like to be, but, well, times have changed and you just can't take the law into your own hands when the future of a whole planet is at stake."

"Spoken like a true lawyer!" I spat back. "Are we supposed to be friends?" I asked, grinding my teeth.

"Well, we're supposed to be ... least ways your daddy and I were," he replied. "But, look, you're a fine Marshal and you've done a lot of good on the job, but, I gotta say, those old books you been filling your head with, especially since Josephine died, and now this mess ... I think you just need a good long rest to sort things out and understand *who* you are and *where* you are."

"Oh, c'mon, Matt," Sam spoke up, "you can't be serious? You want 'em to arrest Wyatt?" Josie just sat there silently and listened.

"No, no I don't, but I don't think I can stop it, legally anyway ... my hands are tied," Mathew lamented, sighing as he heavily flopped into a chair. "The only way out I see is for Wyatt Earp here to resign as Marshal, turn in his badge, and just promise to disappear ...."

"Disappear?" Josie repeated in disbelief.

"Yes," Mathew continued, more tired than angry, "disappear. In other words just go back home Wyatt, you and your kid. Live out your lives quietly and put the past behind you. Maybe they'll accept that as compensation and drop the charges."

Mathew sat back and ran a handkerchief over his sweaty forehead. This was followed by a long period of awkward silence in the room, until finally the doctor spoke up.

"This man," she said, pointing at me, "is not going anywhere in his current condition. His lungs are much too damaged for the length of travel they're suggesting, even in a MEDI Transport. And besides, I have yet to establish, beyond all reasonable medical doubt, that he is not also suffering from lead poisoning and the loss of his marbles," she finished stoically ... then she looked down at me and winked.

I couldn't help myself. I started to belly laugh so hard that the doctor had to call for a couple of white clad aids to sedate and move me back to my hospital room for, as she called it, 'further observation.'

She followed me out of the room, but stopped suddenly at the exit doors to say over her shoulder, "I would strongly advise you initiate a plan to bring this matter to a successful conclusion. I can only, professionally speaking, hold them off for a few more days." She nodded briefly in goodbye, and left as the door slid softly closed behind her.

~ 3 ~

A few days did pass, actually four, and then I had a visit from …

"Marshal Wyatt Earp?" a tall uniformed man asked as soon as he entered my room.

"That's me," I replied.

"I'm here to inform you that you are soon to be released into my custody for transport to a holding facility at North DOME, Adelaide City, pending a disciplinary hearing before the Planetary Board of Inquiry," he said in a very official sounding voice.

"You don't say," I replied, coughing slightly. "Well, sir, I guess that depends on what my doctor says about it and …"

"Doctor Xhin has been removed as your attending physician. Another has been assigned, a human doctor to examine you …" he said with a smug smile on his face. He turned to look back at the door, briefly, and then he stepped up closer to the bed and leaned in. "And I have it on good authority that you will be found fit for travel to your new home where a nice warm welcome is waiting for you … and then, most likely, imprisonment on Clive," he said, almost in a whisper.

"Clive?" I replied.

"Oh, that's right, I forgot, you've lost your memory," he said insincerely. "Well, *former* Marshal Earp, Clive is what we call an asteroid orbiting this planet … it's where we send the losers, renegades and anyone else that hinders progress here on Terra Mynos, especially guys like you who think they can disobey orders and be their own law. You and that crazy kid of yours have caused enough problems for us. Personally, I think they outta vaporize the whole lot of ya …"

I didn't realize I hit him until after I did it. My arm just snapped out and connected with his jaw. He went down like a load of fire wood onto the floor.

"Well, there's another nail in my coffin, I guess," I said into the room.

Just then the door slid sideways and Sam, along with Josie walked in carrying a box.

"What the ..?" Sam blurted in surprise, seeing the body on the deck.

"Daddy, what happened?" Josie asked, hurrying up to the bed.

"He fell," I said.

“Fell?” Sam replied in disbelief, “fell on your fist. Is that about right?”

Josie rolled her eyes and sighed heavily. I had nothing to say.

“This guy’s a government cop. You hit a fellow lawman,” Sam complained.

“I hit a disrespectful thug and I ain’t apologizin’ for it,” I fired back.

“Oh swell,” Sam said, walking around the room, “now what?”

“Now we get daddy outta here,” Josie said. Then she turned to me, “All bets are off. Mathew tried to reason with City Hall, they ain’t buyin’ nothin’ we’re tryin’ to sell … even your resignation won’t do. They want your head in a basket.”

“Yeah, that’s right. Matt said there’s something fishy goin’ on about all this,” Sam added, “he told us to get ya outta town, pronto.”

“So, let’s get!” I said and slipped out of the bed. But my legs had other ideas and didn’t seem to wanna work. I went down.

“Daddy!” Josie yelped as she came round the other side of the bed and tried to help me up.

“I’m okay, girl, just gimme some room,” I growled, as I bullied myself up to a standing position. “Now, where’re my clothes?”

“Here,” Sam said, holding out the box which

contained suitable outdoor clothing and foot wear. I accepted Josie's help getting dressed and we were just about to make our escape when the fella on the floor started comin' around. To my surprise, Josie, without hesitation, hurried over and clocked him a good one, knocking him out cold again. She walked back shaking her hand in the air and wincing in pain.

"Looks like I'm outta practice. We'd better git," she said, heading out the door.

I looked over curiously at Sam. "Don't look at me," he replied defensibly, "she's your kid."

We found an elevator and took it down to the ground level floor. After we landed, we walked as quickly as we could and were just about to the lobby when we heard a voice from behind us.

"Going somewhere?"

We all stopped and turned to see Doctor Xhin walking towards us carrying a cloth satchel. She stopped in front of us and looked at each one. Then, smiling politely, she spoke. "Take this and make sure your father follows the instructions I've included in this kit," she said handing the bag to Josie.

"Yes, ma'am," Josie replied.

"And you help," she said, looking at Sam.

"Uh, sure. No problem," Sam agreed.

"And *you* let them," she said, pointing a finger directly at me.

"More therapy?" I asked.

"Until you're fully recovered, yes ... or else."

"How 'bout my memory," I asked.

"Be patient," Xhin replied.

"I'm no longer a 'patient' here. Thanks for the help, Doc, but we gotta go," I said, pumping her hand in goodbye and now noticing, for the first time, that her kind didn't have a little finger, just three long ones and a thumb. It felt strange, but, even still, she had a firm grip.

We all headed through the cavernous lobby and outta side door to a waiting skimmer hovering a few inches off the pavement. We climbed aboard and took off at ground level for a few hundred yards, then rose to merge with the buzz of fast moving air traffic overhead.

"Wyatt, meet Calvin Hobbs, one of the hands that take care of the compound. I invited him up here to help with your escape," Sam said by way of introduction to the driver. Hobbs looked back briefly and nodded.

"Do I know 'em?" I whispered to Josie.

"You do now," she replied. "He's good people and he knows how to get us outta town without a lot of noise."

"Noise?" I asked.

"Yes, that's a term we use when we track a vehicle,

whether on the surface or in space. Mechanical vehicles leave an energy signature that can be scanned and identified by Law Enforcement, or anyone for that matter, with the right equipment, even a skimmer like this," she explained.

"So, you're sayin' we can be followed by a posse?" I replied.

"Not this crate," Hobbs remarked, twirling a toothpick between his lips, "this baby has been modded real fine, no footprint, period. Good for smuggling contraband ... err, not that I would ever do such an 'illegal thing' mind you," he said, returning to his driving.

Josie smiled at him and turned back to her father. "We're invisible, for now, it just depends how bad they want you and how much man power they want to expend to bring you in."

"Hopefully, I'm not worth it," I remarked, fingering the swath of tape that wrapped up my mid-section.

"Does your wound hurt?" Josie inquired.

"Nah, itches mostly," I lied in reply. "That native doctor did a good job of patchin' me up."

"Well, let's hope we won't be needin' her services any time soon," Josie sighed.

"Who's 'we'?" Sam said. "Knowing Wyatt we'll have bullets pitched at us soon enough ... or worse."

"There's worse?" I asked.

"Oh, don't listen to him, daddy, he's prolly just hungry," Josie said.

"Yeah, so? I miss home cookin' is all. Hope you appreciate this, Wyatt, now that we're *all* fugitives ... hell, I'll probably lose my badge and my pension right along with yours!"

"Does he always whine so much?" I asked.

Josie just giggled and didn't reply.

"So, what's our next move?"

"Gettin' outta Dodge!" Hobbs said.

"Alright, what's 'outta Dodge'?"

"Off world ... at least for the time bein'," Hobbs said.

"Uh, hang on, what's 'off world'?" I asked, without really wantin' to know the answer.

"He means off this rock, this planet," Sam replied. "They'll be lookin' for us back at the compound if they want us that bad ... best to stay away for a spell ... you got us a transport do ya, Hobby?"

"Yep, all arranged," Hobbs smiled back at them as he made a sharp, diving left turn and banked away from the line of traffic, as he headed for one of the many exits to the outside world beyond the protective bubble they were in.

"Wait," I said, "I thought we couldn't go outside because of the 'rads' or some nonsense?"

“No worries, daddy, we’re safe in this particular skimmer. It’s designed for the outer atmosphere, and besides, we’re at high latitude, so the radiation is much less here than down where we found you,” Josie confirmed.

“And where we work!” Sam added.

“South Rim?” I said.

Josie smiled. “That’s right! Are you beginning to recall anything?”

I scratched the stubble on my face. “No, sorry, darlin’, I just remembered that from our conversations. Uh, another thing, how’re we gettin’ ‘off world’ again?”

“Hobby has arranged for us to be passengers on an outbound freighter … at least I assume it’s a freighter?” Josie said, looking over at the driver. Hobbs just smiled and nodded.

“So, where’s it goin, Hobby?” Sam asked.

“*Paulo Mynos*,” Hobbs replied.

“Where’s that?” I asked.

“It’s the smallest of the Mynosian moons. There’s a few scattered settlements, and ore mining operations where there’s pockets of atmosphere,” Josie replied. “How soon do we leave?” she asked Hobbs.

“Soon as we get there. Hang on!” he warned.

Hobbs hit the accelerator and the vehicle shot forward causing everyone to be pushed back into their respective seats. I swallowed hard and tried to keep what little food I still had in my stomach from escaping.

Soon we arrived at what appeared to be a gate leading to the outside and we had no trouble passing the check point before going through the magnetic curtain that acted as a barrier between the city and the raw atmosphere of the planet beyond. The skimmer ran along just above the ground, passing other vehicles of various sizes and uses, both beside and above them.

"Folks live outside the DOME do they?" I asked.

"Some choose to," Josie replied. "The more hearty ones that is ... prospectors, miners, the rough and tumble of humanity, I suppose. It's not easy outside, the air is thinner and the gravity is more. It's a struggle to get around for sure, but you never seemed to mind it," she said, looking closely at me.

"Really?" I said. "How's that?"

"Well, apparently we're from good stock and we adapt quickly," she smiled.

"She's a lot like you, Wyatt," Sam said. "She's got your gumption. I just as soon stay in a unit while on patrol and get out only when I have to."

"In fact, you enjoyed, I mean, enjoy riding your mount without an outdoor suite or ResparAID ... just like the Old West," Josie added.

"I have a horse?" I replied.

"Well, not like you imagine," Josie said. "It's a local animal, like the one they brought you outta the desert on. It's called a ..."

"*Mugwhat*?" I finished for her.

"Yes! That's good," Josie laughed and then hugged me.

"Look darlin', there's nothin' wrong with my short term memory as far as I can tell, it's the long distance stuff that confounds me. So these six legged lizards, I have one do I?"

"Yes you do, and you were very fond of her too," Josie said.

"Were?"

She and Sam looked at each other.

"Uh, she took a few slugs, Wyatt. The search party found her in the desert, she didn't make it," Sam answered carefully.

I rubbed my forehead trying to shake a memory loose. "I wish I could remember the critter," I said. "But, I don't ... sorry."

"It's okay," Josie said. "When this mess is all behind us you can breed another one just like her ... we have her DNA."

"Her what?" I asked.

By this time the skimmer was slowing down and gliding into what looked like a huge metal opening in the side of a mountain.

"We're here, the North-Port Shipping Hanger. This is where we get on the transport for *Paulo Mynos*," Josie said. The skimmer turned on lights and entered the gaping maw of semi-darkness, then followed a row of guide-lights into the interior of the hanger.

It wasn't long before we found ourselves strapped into rough metal seats in an aft cargo hold along with tied down stacks of freight and some pretty noisy wildlife.

"What're they, chickens?" I asked, trying to turn my head enough to get a better look.

"Kinda, I guess," Josie replied as she tightened her straps.

"Lift-off commencing in five ... four ... three ..." a voice blared throughout the cavernous interior.

"Hang on daddy!" Josie said as she closed her eyes.

"Hang on fer what?" I stupidly replied ... and that's when my stomach dropped down into my boots. I remember swearing, then cussing, then imploring the name of Jesus ... then my lungs ached to the point where I couldn't catch my breath ... then I musta blacked out ...

When I came to, Josie was shaking me gently. "Daddy! Daddy, wake up," I heard her voice echo at me from what seemed like far away. I roused myself up to a sitting position on what appeared to be a dock of some sort. I could see my breath. All around me was the bustle of mechanical traffic. Machines with minds of their own it seemed, moving freight from the small to the gigantic in and out of the massive warehouse we were in.

“Daddy, can you walk?” Josie said as she knelt next to me.

“Yeah, c’mon, Wyatt, we gotta skedaddle,” Sam added. He stood, donned in a heavy overcoat with what appeared to be a gunny sack slung over one shoulder, and looked nervously around the place for any ‘human’ observers.

“I think so,” I replied, unconvinced of my ability to actually stand .... But stand I did, with great ease and surprise. “Feels different here,” I said happily as I walked around and stretched the kinks out.

“It’s the lower gravity,” Josie stated. “You’ll probably be able to get around better here than on Mynos. By the way, how do you feel?”

“Not bad,” I said, “wound feels alright too,” I lied; it was still pretty tender.

“Good!” Sam said, “let’s get a move-on before we’re checked by any local security hangin’ around.”

I agreed and the three of us headed down a service ramp that led to a sliding walkway to an exit. Once outside, the air was crisp and still. I looked up and was awestruck by what I saw.

“My God, will ya take a look at that ...” I said.

Above us, taking up a good portion of the sky, hung the massive ball of Terra Mynos 1, the reds, golds, and yellows of its surface moved by slowly in stark contrast to the blackness of infinite, twinkling space that filled the rest of the sky with a rich bed of stars that seemed right at your fingertips. I just stood there and couldn't move as my mind attempted to take it all in.

"It is beautiful, isn't it?" Josie said quietly as she stood next to me rubbing the chill out of her arms.

"I've never seen the like," I replied. I turned physically around several times to gather it all.

"You ain't never been off world. Said it was a waste o-time," Sam said, looking over his shoulder.

"I musta been an idiot," I muttered out loud.

"Nah, daddy, just busy," Josie said. "C'mon let's go, I'm gettin' cold," she urged.

"Yeah, we're wastin' time," Sam said. "Oh, hang on, I almost forgot," he added, as he put down the sack, untied one end and reached inside.

"Bring a lunch, did ya?" I wisecracked.

Sam grunted at the humor as he pulled something out. I recognized it at once.

"We figure you might need this," he said, handing it to me. It was a leather gun belt lined with bullets, and sleeping in the holster was my familiar Colt. I smiled and took it, unhooking the buckle so I could wrap the rig around my waist and synch it snug. I pulled the Colt, examined the action, spun it 'round my trigger finger a few turns and then let it slide back into its sleeve.

“Well, I see you haven’t lost your touch,” Sam smiled as he pulled out another rig and buckled it onto his own waist. Finally, he handed Josie a smaller version of the six-shooter which she slid under her overcoat, behind her belt at the small of her back.

“Are we expecting trouble?” I asked.

“Wyatt, consider this place ‘the frontier’ … Tombstone,” Sam said. “There’s little or no law here, but it’s a good place to hide out until Matt, back planet-side, can figure a way outta this mess for us.”

“And he will,” Josie added.

“In the meantime, let’s go,” Sam said as we continued our walk beyond the buildings. “Hobby gave me a name of a guy here that’s supposed to help us.”

I couldn’t take my eyes off the sky overhead …. so vast and …

“Hey, easy!” Sam said as I bumped into him.

“Sorry,” I apologized, prompting the other two to look at each other oddly.

“That’s a first,” Sam said briefly.

“First fer what?” I asked.

“Uhh, never mind,” Sam quickly replied. “C’mon we’re burnin’ daylight.” He turned and walked away at a quick pace.

“Daylight, it’s still dark,” I said to Josie.

“Not for long,” Josie replied as we walked. “Soon as this rock gets to the other side of Mynos up there, we’ll be in sunlight pretty quick.”

“No domes here?” I asked, looking around.

“Nope, don’t need ‘em,” Sam said over his shoulder as we stepped up on to what looked like a sidewalk that snaked its way down a small hill and into a group of structures. “The atmos is pretty good here, what little there is of it; oh and somethin’ else ...”

With that, Sam took a short run and jumped. He seemed to catapult into the air for an unusual distance before landing on his feet, yards away from us, in the soft dirt next to the walk way. He stood up straight, put both his hands on his hips and laughed.

“I almost forgot how much of a-hoot low-grav is!” he chuckled.

“What in the world?” I skeptically said as we came closer.

“It’s the lower gravity here, daddy,” Josie reminded me. “Easier to walk, run, breathe ...”

“Well, I’ll be,” I said, shaking my head.

“Let’s get inside somewhere,” Sam suggested as he struck out ahead of us.

We all walked quickly to keep up with Sam’s long stride. We finally stopped at a door with a sign awkwardly hanging from a chain above it. ‘Happy Solar Saloon’ it read.

"This is the place," Sam remarked, as he pushed on a pressure plate set into the wall. The door hummed, and then slid to the side. We entered, parting a curtain of heavy Plastoid strips into a dimly lit room with a bar on one end. The air was heavy with smoke from what appeared to be a wood stove set in the middle of the floor. That, along with several of the patrons having cigars stuck into their faces as they puffed, playing cards and sucking down the local brew.

"Smells like an arm pit in here," Josie whispered, as we moved into the room towards the bar. We stood there and waited as several of the customers gave us sideways glances, but said nothing. Then the bartender came over, belched loudly around his cigar, and asked us what we wanted.

"Three beers and the whereabouts of a Jack Quinn," Sam said, as he fiddled around in his pockets for some credits.

"Yeah, well, I got the beers," the bartender rumbled, "but Jack Quinn's another thing ... friend of yours is he?" he asked, chewing on his cigar.

Sam looked around at us. We shrugged and then we noticed that several others in the room had now stood up and were watching us suspiciously.

"Uh, look, Mister," Josie said. "We were given the name by a mutual friend, Cal Hobbs back on Mynos ... but if he ain't here, well, then we'll just take the beers and ..."

“Maybe you’ll get nothin’ little girl,” the bartender threatened as he put both of his beefy hands on the bar top.

“And maybe we need to show these strangers it ain’t polite to come in here and ask questions,” one of the patrons behind us announced. He was a big, bearded man wearing a hat and a weapon tucked behind his belt. The rest mumbled in agreement.

“We ain’t seen a pretty woman ‘round here in a spell either,” another voice in the room said. “Maybe she’s a good breeder?” replied another voice that now encouraged subdued laughter in the place.

“Now, look,” Sam said, clearing his throat, “we don’t want any trouble …”

“Shoulda thought-a that before you landed here,” the bearded man said, stepping forward several paces.

I can’t say I understood what happened next, but a second later my gun appeared in my hand and I fired at the bearded guy. I figured I put a new part in his hair and he was gonna need a new hat. Then I grabbed the bartender behind his fat head, shoved the gun barrel into his mouth, and cocked back the hammer.

“Next shot ventilates what few brains you got!” I threatened. Both Sam and Josie now had their weapons in hand and were nervously pointing at no one in particular in the place. The bartender grunted around the barrel and nodded frantically. “Now,” I said between my teeth, “the man asked you a question, where’s Jack Quinn?”

"He's right here," a voice said from the back of the room.

I turned to see a man walk outta the shadows, step over the bearded guy on the floor holding his head, and come up close to the three of us.

"So, you're the crew Hobby sent up here, huh? You can probably let him go now," he said, lookin' at me with a slight grin.

"Probably so," I replied, pulling the barrel outta the bartender's mouth and then shoving his face hard enough for him to land sprawled out on the dirty, wet floor. "You just stay there 'till we leave, got it?" I ordered him.

"Yes, sir ..." he wheezed and didn't move.

"You can put the hardware away too; I think the show's over, right boys?" Quinn said, turning halfway to the crowd behind him. There were muttered curses of agreement as a few picked up the wounded man and hauled him out. The rest went back to their cards and drinks.

"Well, you must be Earp?" he said, looking at me.

"I guess I must be," I replied.

Jack Quinn was a good lookin' young fella, about Josie's age, with an over confidant swagger about him. He was dressed in a vaguely familiar way. He wore a long, high collared coat that dragged the floor. It reminded me of the 'Dusters' I had read about in my books. The ones the old cowboys wore while riding out on the range. He also wore a large brimmed hat to complete the old west look.

"Sorry about this," he apologized, "it's just folks here aren't used to strangers askin' questions. Let's get outta here before that guy's pals come back," Quinn suggested.

"Fine with us," Sam said, as Quinn turned and headed for the back of the place.

I put Josie between Sam and me and we followed Quinn outta the room, through another door, and into a hall way which led to another corridor that snaked its way down and then turned right. The ceiling was lined with Lumin Strips that cast all of us in an eerie shade of green.

"The buildings are all connected by tunnels," Quinn said, while he walked on ahead of us, "saves dressin' for the sunlight."

"The sunlight?" I said. Quinn turned and looked at me curiously, but kept moving forward.

"I'll explain later, daddy," Josie said behind me.

Eventually we came to a door, entered, and climbed a set of stairs upward to another entrance and another dingy room.

"Well, this is it," Quinn said. "Your home away from home. You'll be safe enough here, for now anyway."

"Yeah, thanks," Sam said as he walked around and looked the place over.

“Yes, thank you, Mr. Quinn,” Josie said.

“Oh, you can call me Jack,” he said sweetly.

“And you can call me her father,” I said, stepping between ‘em.

“Oh, that’s fine, Mr. Earp ... no foul intentions on my part,” Quinn said as he backed away. “It’s just been awhile since I’ve laid eyes on a pretty girl though,” he added, winking at Josie.

“What’re we in to you for anyway?” Sam interrupted from across the room.

“Oh, don’t worry about credits. Hobbs is covering my end. You folks just stay quiet, keep yer heads down and wait it out,” Quinn said, “and I would probably stay away from the Happy Solar,” he added.

“Yeah, no kiddin’,” Sam replied.

“Oh, before I forget,” Quinn said, going over to an old trunk against a wall and opening it, “here’s some outside duds in case you need to leave to buy supplies.

“Outside duds?” I asked.

Sam and Josie went over and pulled out several of the same, tan colored, long overcoats that Quinn wore. On closer inspection, they had a shiny surface that seemed to sparkle even in the dim light.

“Daddy, you wear this over your thermal coat when you go outside,” Josie said holding one up. They pretty well covered up the full length of a man.

“Thermal Coat, huh? Is that what I’m wearin’?” I

felt the fabric of my sleeve.

"It gets pretty cool here, Wyatt, especially at night, with the thin air and all. But the daytime is a bit different," Sam said, accepting one that seemed to fit him.

They also retrieved, out of the trunk, several of the large brimmed hats, along with three pairs of ...

"Sunglasses ... ProTECs are the official name," Josie said, holding up a pair. "You wear 'em to protect your eyes in the daytime. The sun gets pretty bright."

Josie brought over a duster, hat, and sunglasses for me to try on for size and then she outfitted herself.

"Hope you find something that fits," Quinn said. "I tried to be accommodating."

"These'll work, right, Wyatt?" Sam asked.

I nodded as I slipped on the duster over my coat; put on the hat and then the glasses .... I couldn't see a thing.

"They work better outside," Quinn said.

"Well then, let's go outside," I said. "We need food and water if we're gonna stay cooped up in this barn."

"Well, there's a replicator over there," Quinn said, pointing to an appliance sitting on a dirty counter.

Josie went over and fiddled with it. After a few minutes ...

“All it spits out is brown, lumpy gravy,” she said with disgust.

Quinn rubbed his face with embarrassment. “Well then, guess we’d better head over to the supply depot … or I can just go and haul some stuff back.”

“Nope, we’ll all go,” I said, now taking the time to replace the spent cartridge with a fresh one.

“Uh, ya know, the idea is to keep a low profile while you’re here. So far, that hasn’t worked,” Quinn lamented.

“Wyatt’s not one for sittin’ around, are ya, Wyatt?” Sam remarked.

“I don’t hardly think so,” I replied. “Look, Quinn, we appreciate all you’ve done so far, but right now we need some good food and then some good sleep. After that we’ll figure out the best way to keep our heads down.”

“And we need to keep in touch with what’s goin’ on back home too,” Josie added.

“You mean in case they send men after ya?” Quinn asked.

“Think they would?”

“Depends on how hot you are,” Quinn continued. “But I suspect they’ll search planet-side first. I doubt very much they suspect you got as far as here, but ya never can tell. I’ll keep an ear out for ya though.”

“Thanks,” I said. “Now, where the ‘dunny’?”

Quinn chuckled. “Right through there,” he pointed, “first door on the right.”

“Make it quick, daddy, I’m next,” Josie said as I walked away.

After that, we followed Quinn back through the tunnel to a door leading to the outside.

“Mind your eyes, it’s almost sun up,” he said, pulling his hat brim down and putting on his protective glasses. He activated the door and we all stepped through. It was still twilight as I looked around without putting on the glasses. Suddenly, I was surrounded by a blinding, white light as the little moon we were riding on cleared the edge of Mynos 1 and exposed us to the great star beyond. The experience was brief and painful as I quickly shut my eyes and turned my head away.

“Daddy, glasses!” Josie shouted at me. I put them on and carefully opened my eyes. I saw nothing at first, just blackness and for a few long moments I thought it was gonna be permanent, but then I began to see little rows of moving green numbers at each corner of the lenses. Then images started to appear, little by little, until I could see everything clearly.

“You alright, Wyatt?” Sam asked, putting a hand on my shoulder.

“Yeah ... yeah, I guess so,” I replied in relief. “Thought I was blind there for a spell.”

“Keep those on out here or you will be,” Quinn said, “and keep your hands in your pockets or they’ll get sun burnt ... probably should get you folks some gloves while we're at the general store," he added as he moved away towards a row of buildings.

There were a few folks outside wearing similar outfits as they hurried along the streets to where ever they were goin'. I got in line and followed the others to where Quinn was leading us. After we got inside another building, with a sign sayin' 'Supplies,' Josie turned to me and said, "Feel behind your shoulder, if you can reach."

I brought my right hand around, careful of my wound and felt.

"*Ouch!* I yelped. "It's hot back there, what the ..."

"That's why we wear these," she said, tugging on her duster and tapping her hat, "they reflect the sun's rays away from us and our thermal jackets keep us cool in the day, warm at night. Now, promise me you won't go outside without dressing properly, glasses too; this ain't the Rim back on Mynos."

I sighed down at her. "Yep, I hear ya, girl," I replied.

"You'd better," she grumbled. Sam overheard and smiled.

"Shut up you," I said to him. Sam chuckled, turned away and held both hands up.

"Over here folks!" Quinn called from somewhere in the cluttered store.

The three of us wove our way through a maze of

narrow aisles of supplies, stacked boxes and crates. The place seemed to have everything a frontier mining town could want.

"Over here," Quinn shouted again. We came out into an open space and saw Quinn leaning against a counter ... and he wasn't alone. He tossed me a pair of what looked like leather gloves, "Try those on for size. Tell Billy here if they don't fit, and what you need for grub, and he'll fix ya right up," Quinn said, pointing with his thumb to the man standing behind the counter.

"Friends of yours?" Billy, the storekeeper, asked, scratching his big belly.

"Investors up from Mynos ... gonna show 'em around," Quinn lied.

"Investors, huh?" Billy replied, unconvinced. "Well, ya better keep 'em in yer pocket. There was a raid last night over near Preacher's Gulch .... Heard from Charley that they hit the supply depot, the lab *and* the refinery, took a-lotta parts, tools, the usual."

"Anybody hurt?" Quinn asked.

"Nah, just a few bumps and bruises ... couple guys got a shot off or two, I guess. Folks are real edgy this morning about strangers."

"Uh, yeah, we sorta found that out," Sam replied.

"So, what'da ya folks need anyway?" Billy asked us.

"How 'bout a new replicator?" Josie said.

"Sorry, little lady, won't have one for a few weeks. Anythin' else?"

"Yeah," I said, "Who hit your depot and the other places?"

Billy looked over at Quinn almost as if he was asking permission.

"Outlaws," Quinn answered for him. "They've been visiting us here and on some of the other moons and rocks for years."

"Judas Long?" I asked.

Billy started to choke on his own spit as he excused himself and went to fetch some water, or something stronger. Quinn smiled as he watched him leave. "Not likely," he replied, "although it could've been members of his so-called 'gang.' They run quite an operation out here."

"But he's the boss of the outfit, right?" I asked.

"So people say ... why're you so interested anyway?"

"Let's just say I've had some dealings with him in the past and would like to get reacquainted."

Now it was Quinn's turn to cough, and then laugh. "Listen, Mr. Earp, you'd better get that kinda thinkin' outta your head. You and your family here are uninvited guests, even more so after that gunplay last night. My advice to you all is to stay low, keep quiet, and wait out whatever's goin' on against you back planet side. Otherwise, you better be thinkin' of finding another rock to squat on. Push comes to shove you can always try your luck on *Eos* or in the asteroid fields ... better than prison on Clive I suspect. Besides, Judas Long is a ghost, a legend; nobody's actually seen him in years, *if* he ever existed at all."

"You never met him?" Sam asked.

Quinn laughed more. "Well, if I have, I wouldn't know it. I meet a lot of people, but I try to steer clear of pirates."

"You call 'em pirates?" Josie asked.

"Pirates, outlaws, renegades, misfits, it's all the same. They're tryin' to survive in this system just like the rest of us."

"By raiding and killing innocent people?" Josie replied, somewhat offended.

"Well, I'm not sayin' it's right ... don't misunderstand," Quinn backpedaled. "Look, maybe these negotiations I been hearin' about planet side will put all this bad blood to rest."

"You seem to hear a lot. We only found out about the talks just before we left Mynos," Josie said.

"Well, that's my job, little lady, to be nosy *and* in the know," Quinn smiled. "Now, how 'bout we make a list, get supplies and then we'll head back to your quarters."

"How 'bout we make a list and then go visit Preacher's Gulch," I countered.

“Uh, look here, Wyatt,” Sam interrupted, “we got no Peace Officer Status in this town or on this rock, we’re just ‘investors,’ ‘tourists’ or ‘green horns.’ How ‘bout we just hunker down like we were told to and wait for Mathew back home to work things out for us?”

“Then you and Josie stay in the room,” I replied sternly, poking a finger into Sam’s chest. “But Mr. Quinn and I are taking a little ride out to Preacher’s Gulch, aren’t we, Mr. Quinn?” I said, looking over at him. Quinn’s faced turned slightly red, but he smiled quickly and nodded.

“You sure like to cause trouble, don’t ya, Mr. Earp?”

“Seems to come natural,” I said. “Now, let’s get goin’.”

~4~

As it turned out, Sam and Josie refused to stay 'in the barn,' if you will, so we all hopped into a land rover (a six-wheeled contraption) and made the long bumpy trip to Preacher's Gulch. That star was blazing white hot overhead, but the bubble that surrounded us cut the glare enough so we didn't need to wear goggles as we rode.

It was towards noon when we arrived at the mining camp. It looked like a typical Old West town (at least in my mind) ... no domes or fancy structures with slide-doors, just wood frame buildings (artificial wood, Quinn told us) slapped together with good, old fashioned nails.

We got outta the Rover, put our eye ProTECs on and started walkin' to one of my favorite places ... the saloon. Once we got inside, several of the patrons welcomed us (a change from the last place). The bar tender was a good lookin' woman, underdressed to fit the surroundings, and she seemed to know Quinn real well. She slapped him a good one when he got close enough.

"That's fer standin' me up, jackass!" she cussed at him. Quinn faked being embarrassed, rubbed his sore cheek and smiled at her.

"Oh now, Flo, I sent ya a gift .... Look, I had'a leave ... business! I'll make it up to ya, I promise," Quinn explained.

"What gift?" Flo fired back, ramming her hands on her hips.

"Oh, er, well, I'll send you somethin' later, but look, these are my friends from planet side here to look around. They're investors lookin' to buy shares in this dump, maybe. Say, how're the hauls lately?"

"Ore aplenty, as usual," Flo replied, seeming to brighten up. "Say, you folks look thirsty, how 'bout some cold beers? It's on Jack here," she smiled and began to draw three drafts.

"That's fine, ma'am, thank you," Josie said.

"Why aren't you a sweet little thing!" Flo replied. "Are ya old enough to be away from yer momma?"

"Been away from her for a long time. This is my daddy though," Josie said, putting a hand on my shoulder.

"Pleased to meet you, ma'am," I said. We shook hands and then she handed me a beer.

"Flo, this is Sam," Josie said.

"Oh, boyfriend?" Flo smiled.

Sam turned beet red. "Oh, no, ma'am," he replied hastily. "I'm kinda a ..."

"Big brother," Josie finished for him.

"Uh, yeah," Sam said. "I'll have one of those too, ma'am."

Flo handed Sam and Josie a beer. We stood around and enjoyed some small talk, while Quinn went over and chatted with a few of the other customers that decorated the place.

"So, you're 'investors,' huh? Family business?" Flo asked, sipping on a whisky and looking at me over her glass.

"Somethin' like that," I said.

"Hmm, if you say so ... but I've been tending in this dump for almost twenty spins and I ain't never seen an 'investor' haulin' a fancy rig like that," Flo said, pointing to my holster and gun that was showing through my open duster. I pulled the long coat back over it and continued to nurse my drink. The air seemed to get a little thick until Josie spoke up.

"Actually, we're here about that raid that happened recently," she boldly said. Then the whole room got quiet.

"Oops, my fault!" Quinn interrupted suddenly with a laugh, "I ran my big mouth off and now these tourists, I mean, investors wanted to have a look … just curiosity, nothin' serious." Quinn chuckled, trying to make light of it all.

"Actually ma'am," I said to Flo, "I'm lookin' for Judas Long."

Now everyone in the place acted like they had critters in their boots at a funeral. A few quickly put their outdoor gear on and left, while others just looked at each other like somebody had cut wind. Quinn swore under his breath, lifted his hat and ran a hand through his dark hair.

Flo's eyes narrowed. "Why ya want 'em?" she asked, still sippin' on her drink.

"I'm gonna drill a-hole right between his eyes," I replied looking straight at her.

Sam began lookin' for the exit. Josie chewed on her bottom lip and ran her eyes over the ceiling while Quinn plopped down, hard, into the nearest chair.

"Well, mister, you don't mince words do ya?" Flo remarked as she put her empty glass on the bar.

"Nope," I replied. "Has he been here?"

Flo sighed heavily and ran the back of her hand across her mouth. "What makes you think a man like Judas Long comes to this place?" she asked. There was a slight quiver in her voice.

"Because I would," I replied.

Flo laughed. "His boys just hit this town! Took

most of the Tech we need to run our operations. So why would he hang around?"

"Because I would," I repeated. "Now here's what I think is goin' on," I continued, "I think this is perfect base to have a hideout. It's small, isolated, no law, ideal for hiding a ship or ships and there's easy access to planet side. Now, if I were a smart outlaw, like Long, I'd hit my own town every so often just to throw off any suspicion."

"You a lawman are ya?" she asked, leaning forward.

"Colonial Marshal," I said.

"Former," Sam blurted out the side of his mouth.

"Oh God...." Josie sighed.

Flo laughed out loud. "So, lemme get this straight. You're a defrocked lawman out here on some sort of a vendetta against Judas Long?"

"Close enough," I replied simply.

"And what makes you think *I* would know his whereabouts?"

"Because you're his girl," I said.

Several more patrons in the room cleared out.

Flo just stood there and crossed her arms over her mostly exposed chest.

"And how do ya figure that?" she asked sarcastically.

"That tattoo on your left puppy stickin' out there ... the letters: J.D... dead giveaway," I replied. Both Josie and Sam came over to take a closer look. Flo looked either embarrassed or caught as she stuffed herself back into her shirt.

"Quinn, what kinda double-cross is this!" she shouted angrily over at the seated man. Quinn jumped up as if he'd sat on a tack.

"Double-cross! Stuff a boot in your mouth, Flo, I ain't double-dealin' anyone. It's not my fault Wyatt Earp has some brains," he shouted back in defense.

"Wyatt Earp?" Flo exclaimed with genuine surprise on her face. "The Marshal outta South Rim, planet side? You brought him *here*?" she shouted. She reached under the bar and pushed a button ... and then a gun appeared.

The rest of the customers scattered like rabbits as Flo started shootin' ... first at me, then at Quinn, to cover her escape as she backed up behind the bar, firing randomly as she moved toward a curtain in the wall.

As soon as I saw the weapon, I hit the floor dragging Josie with me. Sam jumped over a table, pulled his gun and got off a round at the retreating bartender. Quinn took a slug in the shoulder, fell over his chair and banged his head. Then more shots were fired from behind the curtain as Flo turned and hurried through, yelling orders at someone. By this time, I was on my feet, Colt in hand and quickly fanned three shots through the curtain. Seconds later a man fell forward, face first, onto the floor.

"Sam!" I shouted. Sam seemed to understand what I wanted, and hurried over to cover Josie while I headed for the curtain.

"Daddy, don't you dare leave us behind again!" Josie screamed at me. I pulled up short, arm straight out, gun cocked as I walked slowly to the bullet-ridden curtain. I stuck the barrel through and parted them, but all that greeted me was an empty hallway. I turned back to look at them both huddled on the floor, Sam with his weapon drawn and his arm tight around Josie who had flames in her eyes. Then I knelt down beside the dead man and turned him over. I had put three into him. He lay there staring back at me. Quinn groaned from across the room where he rolled back and forth in pain, clutching his shoulder on the dirty floor.

"Better see to him," I said.

Sam let Josie go and went to Quinn. Then Sam came over and knelt beside me. I just stared back at the dead man like he wasn't real. Sam reached down and moved his eyelids closed.

"You okay, Wyatt?" he asked.

"Have I done this before, Sam?"

Sam sighed heavily and put a hand on my back. "Yep, out there in that desert ... and before that, when necessary. So did our daddies. You want Judas Long or what?"

I looked at Sam. "I made a promise to myself in that hospital and today to that bartender. Maybe I was a better, harder man before I lost my marbles, but I'm still Wyatt Earp and I'm gonna get the man that killed my wife and that child's momma."

"And I'm gonna help ya," Sam replied. "Now let's go."

We got Quinn to his feet. He was leaking blood at a pretty good rate and he looked like he was fixin' to pass out. I slapped his face several times to get him to come around.

"You gotta doc in this town? Quinn, answer me!" I barked.

"Yeah, out the front, take-a right, three doors down," he managed to get out before he went limp. Sam bent him over a shoulder and nodded for us to go ahead out.

"Hats and eye protection," Josie reminded us, as she found Quinn's glasses and put them on him along with his hat. The rest of us did the same. Then we went outside.

The blast of white light took our optics a few long seconds to calibrate to our individual eyes … a few seconds too long, it seemed, as wood chip flew in all directions the moment we cleared the doorway.

"Go right! Hurry!" I shouted at Sam and Josie, "get 'em to the doc's," I ordered.

Daddy!" I heard Josie shout.

"Confounded things," I cursed my glasses as numbers scrolled at the edges but I still had no vision. Then, I took a deep breath, raised my weapon, closed my eyes, listened, and waited as I backed up slowly. After a moment I heard what I was waiting for, a *click*. I fired in that direction and heard a man scream. I continued to walk backward, following the other two. I heard footfalls to my left; I fired again. Someone cursed and ran away. By this time, my glasses had refocused enough for me to see my surroundings. I now saw a man across the street in an alley raise something in his hand. I dropped down to one knee and fanned off two rounds. The Colt roared and the unknown man slid down the wall.

"Daddy!" I heard Josie yell from behind me. More shots were discharged where she and Sam were. I ran toward them, lost my footing, did a complete mid-air flip and landed on my belly.

"What the..!" I cursed. Then I remembered the low gravity. Josie's pistol went off twice while Sam kept tryin' to kick a door in with Quinn dangling from a shoulder. I got up carefully and jumped. I bounded several yards and landed just about where Josie was standing, her arms outstretched, gripping her weapon and looking frantically for a target.

"Josie, go shoot the door! I'll wait here, go!" I ordered. Josie understood and spun around.

"Sam, move!" she yelled.

Sam stood aside as she emptied her weapon into the fake wood, splintering the frame where the dead bolt held the door fast. Now, when Sam kicked it, it gave way.

“Inside!” Sam yelled.

“Daddy, c’mon!” Josie shouted as she followed them in.

I backed up, scanning the buildings beyond for any movement, but all was silent. I crossed the threshold and slammed the door behind me. It was pitch dark in the place, that is, until I took those blasted glasses off. The inside was an office of some sort, but it looked deserted … or so we thought. We heard a cough come from another room. I went to investigate while Josie reloaded her gun. I opened a door and stuck my weapon in first.

“Don’t shoot, Mister!” a voice pleaded.

“Come on out here,” I said, and backed up.

What came through the door was an older man, bald on top with white hair around the rim, and he was wearing what looked like a pair of old fashioned wire spectacles down low on his nose.

“You the doctor?” I asked.

“Why, you hurt?” he replied, nervously.

“No, but he is,” I said, tipping my head toward Sam who still held Quinn draped over his shoulder like an old rug.

“Probably a few more outside too,” Sam added.

"Good lord, bring him in here," the doc said, pointing behind him to an examination table. Sam brought Quinn through and laid him out on the table top, while the doctor stuck both hands under a unit sitting on the counter that sprayed his hands with some kinda stretchy film that acted like gloves. (Josie explained it to me later.)

"Now, let's see what the damage is," he said. Then he abruptly stopped. "Good lord, this is Quinn!"

"So what?" Sam said.

"Nothing," the doc replied, nervously, "Now, you get these clothes off him," he ordered Sam, while he stood there holding his hands up like they were wet. He watched as Sam and Josie removed Quinn's garments 'till he was bare chested.

"Did you shoot him?" he asked Sam.

"Me? No!"

"You?" he accused, looking at me.

"Not yet," I replied. "If you gotta know, it was the bartender, Flo. What's the problem, just fix him."

"Not if he's fighting against ... well, the people who run this place."

"You mean Judas Long and his gang of outlaws?"

"Look, whoever you people are, I don't want or need trouble ... I heard all the shooting outside ... now I like Quinn here, but if he's involved with them, well ..."

“What’s wrong with you old man?” Josie snapped back. “Didn’t you take an oath or somethin’?”

“Well young lady, actually, I’m not an M.D., I’m more of a scientist and ...”

Quinn now decided to come to and began to cry, struggle and flop around.

“Don’t you have somethin’ to sedate him?” Josie asked. “He’s gonna do more damage to himself than the bullet.

“Actually, I’m not sure,” the doctor said, looking around, “we don’t have much call for this kind of injury and ...”

“Oh never mind,” Sam interrupted. “Quinn, you okay?”

“No! I’m dyin’,” he bellowed.

Then Sam hit him, knockin’ him out cold. “Now get to work or you’re next, Doc” Sam threatened.

Josie giggled, and I nodded in approval, as the old man began the task of removing the bullet from Quinn’s shoulder.

An hour or so passed. Sam and I paced between both rooms but kept an eye on the front door. There were windows of a sort in some of the buildings, but they were designed much like our eye-ProTECs. According to Josie they were a light responsive polymer that reduced the sun’s damaging glare. The doctor's office didn't have one, so Sam and I took turns playing 'chicken' … moving the chair we had braced up against the door frame and sticking our heads outside to see who was around. It was still quiet, which made me wonder if Flo and those with her had already high-tailed it off-world. Finally, Josie came out and told us that Quinn would be fine despite the hole in his shoulder and the knot on the back of his head.

"Good," I replied. "Is he awake? 'Cuz we need to talk."

"About what?"

"About what he knows and what he hasn't told us. I think he's up to his neck in all this," I said.

"Daddy, he's wounded," Josie warned.

"Maybe so, but if I find out he's mixed up in getting' us shot at, he'll wish Flo had aimed straighter," I replied.

"Lemme talk to him, will ya?"

"Think a pretty face will work better?"

"Better than threats or worse. Look, I know we're in a jam here, but lemme give it a try before you start shootin'?"

She stood there with her hands on her hips and just for a second in my mind she transformed into an older version, shaking her head at me in a familiar way that I could almost …

"Daddy, are you okay?" I heard her ask.

"Uh, yeah," I replied. "Alright girl, you go have your talk with Quinn, but don't take long. We gotta figure a way outta here."

"Best be waitin' 'till dark," Sam suggested. "Maybe Quinn can work some magic and find us a ship off this rock before we get plugged."

"Yeah, well, I gotta feelin' maybe Mr. Quinn can tell us where Judas Long is. Anyway, go talk to him, Josie, Sam and I'll mind the door," I said.

Josie turned and went back inside the treatment room and shut the door, while Sam and I pulled up a couple chairs in good view of the front door.

"How ya fixed for ammo?" I asked.

Sam checked his gun belt, then his pockets. "I got about a dozen. You?"

"'Bout the same, I guess," I replied, spinning the chamber on my weapon and then placing it in my lap.

"I brought more, back at that rooming house," Sam said.

"Lot of good it's doin' there," I grumbled; so did my stomach.

"I heard that," Sam replied. "We'd better figure a way to get us fed too."

Then the doctor came in.

“Well, looks like the young couple have a great deal to talk about,” he said, pulling up a chair. “And you two have brought trouble we don’t need down on our heads,” he scolded.

“Mister, them two ain’t a ‘couple’ and you bought trouble when you let a gang of outlaws take over this town and use it for a hideout,” I fired back.

The doctor cleared his throat. “Sorry, my mistake. By the way, the name is Adamson, and as far as the ‘outlaws’ are concerned, it wasn’t my decision, I assure you,” he replied, “it seemed better to just cooperate.”

“You shoulda contacted the law planet side,” Sam said.

“I told the town folk that they should, but they wouldn’t listen. Too afraid I guess. Then the others said that if I didn’t cooperate and keep my trap shut I’d become a floater off one of the freighter ore runs.”

I looked over at Sam, confused.

“A ‘floater’ is what pilots call a dead body in space. Criminals sometimes push folks outta air locks. Not a happy way to go,” Sam explained.

“I see. Well, I guess we wouldn’t want that, would we, Doc?”

The old guy just hung his head.

“So who’s ‘the others’?” Sam asked.

“The bunch that run things around here. That female bartender and her boys.”

"You mean Flo?"

"Yes, I mean her. She keeps an eye on things for, well, him."

"You mean Judas Long?"

"Yes."

"He been around?" I asked.

"No, but his men are always here. The rest of us are just about prisoners."

"He run the mines and the lab too?" Sam asked.

"They have their fingers in everything and not just on this rock either. I understand they're trying to take over things planet side too."

"You mean the negotiations?"

"Negotiations? Negotiations my foot!" the old doctor laughed. "That's a clever ruse to get their mitts into the colonial government."

"They wanna run the whole show then, huh?" I said.

"You gotta be kiddin' me?" Sam replied.

"Wish I were ... but there's other concerns more important than who runs what around here," Adamson said.

"Like?"

"Like makin' more human babies for one thing, and fast, otherwise the Menutans will have their planet back."

"Yeah, we heard about that business," Sam said. "But, we were told it had to do with the radiation on the surface and ..."

"No! No indeed," the old doctor replied, raising a finger. "It's system wide. It's that star we're exposed to," he pointed upward, "can't get away from it ... it messes with our reproductive genes on the one hand, and on the other, well ..."

"Well, what?" I asked.

"It increases our life span. If it didn't, why we'd all have been a memory a long time ago."

Sam and I looked at each other trying to make sense of what the old boy just said.

"What'da ya mean, Doc? I'm as old as I would be anywhere else," Sam replied.

Adamson crossed his legs and smiled. "How old do you think you are, son?" he asked.

Sam looked a little confused for a moment, then said, "Why, I'm forty-three, last time I checked."

"How 'bout you, sir?" he said, looking at me.

"About fifty, give or take. What's yer point?"

"You two don't remember the crossing then?"

"Crossing?" we both said.

“Yes, from Terra to here, in the ARK ships.”

Sam and I both started to laugh. “Doc, you been in the thin air too long,” Sam said, slapping a knee, “that happened hundreds of years ago. Wyatt and I, our parents and their parents, *and theirs*, were all born here ... I mean down on Mynos.”

Doctor Adamson just sat there and slowly shook his head as if in pity.

“I’m sorry ... they were supposed to tell you... they were supposed to tell everyone, they promised,” he said. “They never would listen to me and now we’re in this mess,” he rattled on almost to himself.

“Look Doc, you ain’t makin’ sense,” Sam said, “tell us what?”

He looked over at us with great emotion in his eyes as if remembering.

“*I* remember the crossing. I was there and so were you and your families ... we all crossed through the great void together to this new home,” he said, almost religiously.

“What?” Sam and I both said in disbelief.

“You don’t remember. It’s understandable.”

“Well, he doesn’t,” Sam said, pointing at me, “he’s been shot up, beat up and exposed to Rads. His memory is toast, he don’t even remember his own kid. But, there ain’t nothin’ wrong with *my* memory and I don’t remember no ARK ship or space travel. I remember my readin’ about it in the archives and my granddaddy tellin' me what his granddaddy told him ...."

"It's the effect of long term sleep, the Hyper-STASIS we were all under for years ... so many years," Adamson said quietly, more to himself than us.

"Doc, yer nuts!" Sam replied bluntly.

"Hold on partner, let's hear 'em out," I said.

"Look, I know it sounds fantastic, but listen," Adamson said, leaning forward. "The ARK Program was instituted back on Terra because, well, the human race needed to survive its own stupidity and mismanagement. Dozens of families were chosen, at least three generations, to travel to this star system and we did. Then we sent a message in a probe back to Terra, but we never heard a response. So, we made do with what we brought, our science, our Tech and we assisted the native culture with its woes and we became allies sharing this world. They seemed to understand more than we did about the effect of long term space travel and their particular star. It seems that the Hyper-STASIS had a peculiar effect on us that our scientists did not anticipate. It subconsciously skewed our sense of relative time to begin with. Then, the Proxima star actually lengthened our biological lives by, well, double, sometimes more, depending on the individual's gene pool ..."

"Wait, if what yer sayin' is so, then we *all* should be alive, my daddy, his daddy ..." Sam said.

“No,” the doctor said. “The advancing age is proportional. Let me ask, how old was your father when he died?”

Sam scratched his unshaven face. “About eighty-five, I reckon; my wife would know.”

“Sir, he was at least one hundred eighty-five, perhaps more and his father, probably around the same when he died,” the doctor replied with authority. “*We*, that is, our conscious minds, simply don’t register that though ... the passing of this kind of time. The fact is, we were *all* old when we arrived, even the children that left, Terra, but we simply, because of Hyper-STASIS, did not biologically age. And, to complicate things more, our scientist had no idea that this star would *also* contribute to the slowing down of the aging process, and along with that, the birth rate.

“So yer sayin’ we can’t reproduce because we’re all too old?” I asked.

“That’s a factor, but not the only one. It’s also due to radiation exposure; not only on the planet’s surface, but from the star itself ... the science is complicated, but provable by the mere fact that the outlaws who are not living planet-side are not reproducing either.

“So, hold yer horses, Doc,” Sam interrupted, standing up. “Are you tellin’ me I’m ninety years old?”

“Probably older, and mind you, that’s Terran time, not Menutan.”

Sam walked around the room chuckling to himself. Putting his eye protection on, he poked his head out the door, looked around briefly, closed it and repositioned the chair. Then he looked over at me and shook his head.

“Yer awful quiet, boss; what’da you think about what we’re hearin’?”

I stretched, and then crossed my legs.

“Sounds to me like a pretty entertaining yarn to pass the time,” I replied, looking over at Doc Adamson.

The doctor’s face reddened. “Believe me or don’t, I don’t really care,” he responded, obviously hurt. “The scientific facts are all there for even the most credulous to see. Besides, you two, as well as those two in there,” he said pointing to the other room where Josie and Quinn were still talking, “probably won’t have to worry about dying of old age.”

“Why’s that?” Sam asked.

“Once Judas Long gets word of your presence, he’ll return and end all of our lives abruptly,” Adamson replied solemnly.

“We’ll see,” I replied. “How’s it look outside, Sam?”

“Quiet,” he said.

“For now,” the doctor added. “Wait’ll this rock travels behind Mynos in a few hours .... You’re going to need more bullets.”

Just then Josie opened the door and came in. She left it open so we could see Quinn sitting up with his legs dangling off the table and his bandaged arm trussed up in a sling. I looked over at him.

"You gonna live?" I asked.

Lookin' somewhat pale, he responded, "Oh, I suppose," as cheerfully as he could. "Guess ya never know how the day's gonna turn out, huh?"

"You gotta weapon?"

"Yeah, in my jacket. Why, you thinkin' about shootin' our way outta here?"

"Depends. Doc, why don't you examine the boy and make sure he's fit ... give us a few minutes alone," I said.

The old doctor slapped his knees as he rose. "What I told you was the truth," he said, looking down at me. I nodded toward where Quinn sat and Adamson left.

"Close the door, will ya?" I asked. Once the three of us were alone I spoke to Josie. "What'd you find out about young Jack Quinn? Can we trust him?"

"Why daddy? Still itchin' to shoot him?" she replied.

"Don't get sassy girl, I'm not anxious to shoot anyone unless it's to save our necks," I scolded. "Now, we're in a tight spot here and I need to know if Quinn in there is with us or against us."

“Oh, he’s not part of Judas Long’s gang if that’s what you mean,” she replied with a huff as she looked up at the ceiling. Then I noticed something.

“What happened to your neck? You wounded?” I asked, standing up. Now Sam came over.

Josie immediately covered her neck with a hand. “It’s nothin’, just-a scratch ....”

“Lemme see that,” Sam insisted, taking her hand away. After examining the alleged wound, Sam laughed, patted her cheek, then went over and sat down.

“Well?” I said, turning her towards me so I could have a look.

“It sure ain’t fatal … but it could be for someone,” Sam chuckled.

“What is that?” I asked looking at the deep, red mark on Josie’s neck.

“Oh daddy, it’s nothing!” Josie replied, getting upset.

“Tell him Josie, or I will,” Sam said, smiling up at her.

Josie eyes pitched daggers at him. Then she cleared her throat.

“It’s just a … a …”

“Hickey!” Sam guffawed, slapping his knee.

“A what?” I replied.

“Oh c’mon, Wyatt, you know … from suckin’ on her neck.” Sam continued to laugh.

“Are you enjoying this, ya big goof?” Josie snapped at him, trying to control her temper. “You’d better not go to sleep tonight or I swear …”

“What!” I erupted. “You two’ve been spoonin’ in there whilst Sam and I’ve been guarding that door from folks tryin’ to kill us all?”

“Oh, daddy, it’s not what you think … I had’da soften him up some so he’d feel comfortable talkin’, *and* he did, so relax,” she said, defending herself.

“Relax,” I barked, pulling my gun. “I’m gonna ventilate that kid’s head ….”

“Stop it!” Josie said, grabbing me firmly by my shirt with both hands. “Now you listen up. I’m a grown woman and I’ve had to be since momma died. And, I’ve takin’ care of you since that day … with all your moods and living out in the middle of nowhere with nowhere to go except on a computer monitor and I’ll explain what that is later. Now, my options for ever finding a man, *any* man, is looking grimmer the older I get. So, when I run across one that actually likes me and who my father hasn’t shot yet, I’m gonna make-a run at him! And, I’m *not* the only one of us that has a hickey on his neck either, so if you’re gonna shoot him, shoot me too, will ya? Put us both out of our misery!” By the time she was finished she was shouting pretty loud.

I stood there transfixed by the intensity of what came outta her … and my stomach hurt, not only from lack of food, but from embarrassment. I holstered my gun, took her by the shoulders and kissed her on the face. Then I just held her for a few moments tryin' to remember her mother and what a fine woman she musta been.

"I'm sorry, girl," I finally said. "You're right … you gotta right to choose and I won't fault ya for it. Now, lemme ask you, do ya trust him?"

"Yes," she said, her eyes bright with tears.

"Alright, then so do I. Sam?"

Sam rubbed the back of his neck. "Fine with me. I just wanna know what his deal is."

Josie went on to answer that for the next few minutes. When she was finished, she sat down and put her head in her hands. Seems Quinn was orphaned early, moved from mining camp to mining camp on various rocks, and basically raised himself. He discovered he had a real talent and personality for getting people what they wanted, legally or otherwise. He had done some business with Long's crew from time to time, but insisted he was not part of their operation. And he had a real liking for Josie.

"I'm starvin'," Josie said.

"Yeah, me too," I agreed. "Okay, let's see if we can fix that."

I turned and walked into the room where both the doctor and Quinn sat contemplating their immediate future.

"Uh, Mr. Earp," Quinn began as he held his wounded arm, "let me assure you, sir, that my intentions towards your daughter are completely honorable and ..."

"Stop talkin', boy," I said, cutting him off. "Let me just say regarding my daughter that your intentions had better be, or you're a dead man .... That's all I'm gonna say about that. Now, we need food, water and a way outta here before it gets dark. So, how do we go about doin' that?"

"There are some supplies in there," the doctor said, pointing to a cabinet. Josie went over, opened it and found several rows of bottled, recycled water and several containers of dried rations. She took a few of the bottles and handed them out to us. It didn't seem to taste quite right to me, but it was wet.

"Gotta replicator, Doctor?" she asked.

"Yes, there's a small kitchen through there."

He pointed to an entranceway to another small room. Josie went through and returned a few minutes later carrying a tray with several drinking containers of what smelled like chicken soup and a plate of what looked like some form of bread. She passed them among us and then assisted Quinn. The two smiled at each other as they both shared food.

"A last supper," the doctor muttered.

"Say again?" Sam asked.

"Oh ... nothing, nothing, just thinking out loud," he replied as he ate.

"Well," Quinn said, breaking the silence. "The best way outta here is through the tunnels, but, they prolly got' em covered by now."

"How many men they got?" I asked.

"Not countin' the ones you shot, probably a dozen, but I can't be sure, *I'm* not one of 'em."

"Jack, he knows that," Josie reassured him.

"Another thing, the town folk who work the mines aren't the bad guys either. They just cooperate and try to mind their own business."

"Well, let's hope you're right," Sam said. "I don't look forward to havin' the whole town down on us."

"Have any idea where Judas Long lays his head?" I asked.

Quinn shook his head. "Nope and I don't wanna know," he replied between mouthfuls.

"I might be able to help with that," Doctor Adamson said. "As I had mentioned, I'm not actually a medical doctor, but a scientist. I worked at the laboratory that was set up on this moon. We thought, in our ignorance at the time, that it would be safe from the Zeta Radiation. But, it really doesn't matter now since the research has changed ...."

"You know somebody at this lab, do ya, Doc, that's

willin' to help us out?" I asked.

"Perhaps. If you're looking to escape to someplace safer."

"Nope, I'm askin' if you know somebody who can put me in contact with Judas Long."

"You seem to be fixated on getting everyone killed, aren't you? Marshal is it?"

"Somethin' like that," I said. "Look, you don't have to be involved in our business, just put us in touch with someone."

"I became involved when you broke into my office," Adamson said, pointing his finger at me.

"I'll apologize later. Now, about this person?"

"He was a colleague ... working on the project. I believe he knows this Mr. Long."

"What 'project?'" Josie asked as she went around and picked up empty food containers from us.

"Best kept secret," he smiled, vaguely. "Although, I don't suppose it matters now to say ... it might be psychologically beneficial for me to get it off my chest."

Everyone looked strangely at him which only caused the old man to chuckle. "You should see your faces," he laughed, "think I've been out in the sun too long, I suspect .... Well, if you think what I told you earlier sounds fantastic, pull up a chair."

"Hang on, Doc," Sam interrupted. "Shouldn't we be talkin' about gettin' outta here?"

"And go where?" Quinn said. "Apparently we can't leave by the front door."

"Well, I dunno," Sam replied, "I ain't seen nobody in a while. Maybe they took off?"

"Let's find out," Quinn said, grabbing his hat and glasses, then walking out.

"Jack?" Josie said, attempting to follow.

"Stay here, darlin'. I'll be right back," Quinn said.

Quinn walked out to the front door, removed the chair, put his glasses on, opened the door and shoved his hat outside with his good hand holding onto the brim. Immediately, several holes appeared in Quinn's hat. He pulled his arm inside and turned around. The rest had now entered the room as Quinn quickly shut and braced the door behind him. Then he turned and proudly displayed the smoldering holes in his headwear.

"Well, looks like they got the door covered pretty good." Quinn smiled.

"I didn't hear any gunfire," I said.

"Nope, that's 'cuz they prolly got a beam turret set up out there somewhere keepin' an eye on this place," Quinn said, walking over.

"A what?" I replied.

"It's an energy weapon on a tripod, Wyatt," Sam explained. "Fully automatic, if it senses movement, it shoots at it."

"I thought those fancy weapons didn't work here?" I said.

"Only planet side, daddy," Josie corrected.

"They work just swell 'round here," Quinn smiled, sticking his fingers through the holes and wiggling them. "They'll fry ya before you have time to blink."

"So, yer sayin' it's a machine out there doin' the shootin'?" I asked.

"Yup," Quinn said. "And if I was them outlaws, I'd have a couple units set up in the tunnels just waitin' for us to run into 'em."

"Uh, excuse me," Adamson interrupted. "Where're you from anyway?" he said, looking strangely at me.

"Oh, sorry, Doctor," Josie replied. "My father is suffering from a form of amnesia due to an injury. He thinks he's in the 1800's Old West and ..."

"Dadgummit, woman, I know what century I'm livin' in!" I retorted. "I'm just, well, confused about some things, so don't go makin' it worse than it is," I griped.

"Sorry, daddy," Josie said, hugging my arm.

"Fascinating," the doctor replied. "You're probably blessed actually, Mister ...?"

"It's Earp, Wyatt Earp," I replied.

"You're joking?" Adamson said. "You also think

you're a famous lawman?

"No, Doctor, my father *is* Wyatt Earp, a direct descendant. That part is accurate, believe me," Josie replied.

"Well, I'll be," Adamson remarked, "And you want to bring Judas Long to justice …."

"Maybe toes up," Sam interjected.

"Either way, it's a pleasure to meet you," the doctor said, coming over to shake my hand. I felt odd about it, as he took my right hand in both of his and shook. He had the look of a school boy meeting his hero …. My feet started to itch and …

"I'm sorry," he apologized, "it's just that, well, it's gratifying to know that some of our heritage has survived."

"I'm nobody special," I said, feelin' uncomfortable.

"Perhaps you're just the kind of man we need to straighten out this mess," he said.

"So, what kinda work do you do at the lab, Doctor?" Josie asked.

"My field of study includes biological chemistry, among other things … and, well, I used to work at the lab, but I wasn't particularly cooperative regarding the direction the science was taking," he said.

"You said a few minutes ago that the 'research had changed'?" Josie replied.

"Yes. Originally we were set up by the Colonial Scientific Commission to aid in facilitating the Menutan Project, as we called it at the time ... that is, getting their species to be more genetically adaptable to the sudden change in the planet's radiation levels. It seems that this particular world experiences a periodic radiation flux every few centuries or so due to the sun's effect on the planet's magnetic field and ... "

He rambled on like this for a few minutes until I, loudly, cleared my throat.

"Oh, I apologize," he said, "I do tend to go on, don't I?"

"Yup," Quinn grinned.

"So we showed 'em how to build the DOMEs and shared other Tech, right?" Sam said

"Yes, that is correct. And in exchange they helped us in a variety of ways. It soon became a symbiotic relationship that benefitted both our species."

"But now there's a problem?" I asked.

"Well yes, mostly with us. I'm sure you're aware of the under population problem our people are having?"

The rest of us nodded. "It's our star, right, messing with our ability to reproduce?" Josie said.

"Well, yes," Adamson said, "among other things. That's the scientific/medical challenge we have and that's what the lab here, and on some of the other moons and planet side have been trying to figure out. However, it seems that certain people in our government believe that interspecies reproduction is the answer. I'm sure you've heard the controversy about this?"

"Yeah, somewhat," Sam said, "we're kinda isolated from a lot of this talk, living out on the Rim as we do. More of a big city problem to us, well, least it was, I guess ...."

"Not anymore," Adamson replied, holding up a finger, "if you're human, it's a problem. Actually, there's quite a division over this. Divisions in culture, science, personal beliefs, religious convictions, among other things, and these factors have contributed, I understand, to a variety of rather 'Frankensteinish' experiments by some of my former colleagues."

"Who's Frank and Stein?" Quinn asked.

"Good question, boy," I added.

"A monster maker in human popular fiction," the doctor quickly replied. "No matter. The point is I objected to some of the unethical experiments that were being sanctioned by our government."

"Does this have anything to do with mating with the Menutans?" Josie asked.

Adamson sighed heavily. "Yes and no. Genetically, Humans and Menutans share compatibility in this regard. In other words, pregnancy can occur and has occurred."

"Sounds like a way out," I said.

"Yes and no," Adamson repeated, rubbing the back

of his neck. “As I mentioned, there are strong cultural differences on both sides … neither side wants to risk diluting or relinquishing their identity as a species, which, according to present theories would eventually happen as time passed … especially for the human race. We would be absorbed into the Menutan genome.”

“So we would die out as the human race in this star system?” Sam asked.

“Yes, in theory … but there are so many variables that …”

“Well, I’m not nuts about that idea,” Sam replied.

“Me either,” Quinn added.

“Gentlemen, I wouldn’t needlessly worry about that as a certain future since Human and Menutan pregnancies rarely occur and when they do the gestation period is so long that it would be simply impractical to look to this as a viable solution to our population problem.”

“So, now what?” Josie asked.

“Well, other methods of research were implemented that I disagreed with.”

“So, they cut you loose,” I said.

“Well, not at first. I was reassigned here. After awhile though, I discovered that our friends from the other side … the outlaws, as you refer to them, have their own agenda.”

"How's that?"

"The raids they conducted over the years were not just for sustaining their little group, it was to procure equipment, Tech and people, people like me, to do research for them."

"Is that what you did here?"

"Yes, I'm afraid so."

"What kinda research?"

"Genetic duplication," he said carefully.

"You mean cloning?" Josie said.

"Yes."

Josie and Sam both swore at the same time.

"That practice was outlawed back on Terra *and* here, as far as I know," Sam said.

"And that, among other things, was the basis of my disagreement with some of my colleagues back planet side, however, upon my arrival *here*, I found that the science, as instituted by the outlaws, was progressing secretly and rapidly."

"So what'd you do about it?" Josie asked.

"I quit. Just walked away. Now, I'm the town doctor, if you will."

"And these guys let you?" I asked.

"Yes. Does that surprise you? The fact is, the outlaws are not as ruthless as they've been painted.

As a group, they're just as concerned, perhaps even more so, about perpetuating our species in this system than some down on the planet. They just go about it more, shall we say, aggressively."

"By robbin' and killin'?"

"Only if shot at first ... or so I'm told."

"Well, that sure wasn't the case back in the bar," Quinn replied, adjusting his sling.

"There's a few radicals, apparently," Adamson said.

"So, why're you still alive?" I asked.

"Because I'm valuable, at least as a medical man. It's not like we have colleges producing M.D.s ... fact is, there's very few of us left to fix the rest. They understand that."

"Sounds like you admire 'em?"

"I only admire their zeal, not the science. There are inherent problems with clones, as we experienced back on Terra ... people simply were not ready for another race to share dwindling resources."

"I remember my granddaddy tellin' us kids about the conflicts. They said they weren't really 'human.'"

Adamson smiled reflectively. "Yes, those were dark times, but I'd like to think we overcame them like we did other prejudices of the past."

"How far along is the research here?" Josie asked.

"I'm not sure," Adamson said. "I suppose I should

have stuck it out longer to find out, but I didn't. So, I'm uncertain."

Suddenly, there was a loud banging on the front office door!

~5~

"Doc! Ya gotta come quick, we got wounded out here!" someone on the other side of the door yelled.

Sam, Josie and I all drew our weapons at the same time. Doc Adamson held up a hand in caution and approached the door.

"Who's there? What's happened?" he hollered through it.

"Doc, this is Pete, Pete Haskell ... you know I ain't one of them outlaws and no part of them strangers that shot up the place earlier, but, ya gotta come to Lab One, there's been some trouble and we got wounded over there."

"I know this man," Adamson said, turning to us.

"You can let him in, but if he blinks wrong ..." I warned.

“I understand,” the doctor said, and then he moved the chair and opened the door. “Pete, you step inside here and explain.”

The man, Pete, walked in and he seemed to be alone. Once inside, he removed his protective glasses and stared into the muzzles of three guns.

“Oh, I see you fellers, ma’am, are still here,” he said, nervously. “We figured you took the tunnels and lit out by now.”

“What about them turrets?” Quinn asked.

“We disabled them soon as we got wind of the accident over at Lab One. Folks that are still there sent me over to get the Doc here.”

“What happened, Pete?” Adamson asked.

“Well, far as I can tell, when these folks started shootin’ Flo’s boys, they all headed over to the mine to get reinforcements, but there was some kinda scuffle amongst ‘em and then they started fightin’. Some of ‘em came armed into the lab and tried to take some equipment and people to the jump-ship they got hid.”

“They wanted the researchers?”

“I guess, a few of ‘em, and some other stuff they was haulin’, I dunno, all I know is the shootin’ commenced again, only a stray shot touched off somethin’ that exploded. It killed a few, but there’s others that are hurt bad. Can ya come?”

Doctor Adamson looked over at me, and so did everybody else.

“Mister, is Judas Long among ‘em?”

“I’m thinkin’ so, but I can’t be sure,” Pete replied, breathing hard.

“Alright, let’s get!” I said.

Doctor Adamson grabbed an alloy suitcase full of medical supplies from one of the cabinets, then we put on our outdoor gear and followed Pete out of the office, across the street where we all crammed into an old, beat-up lookin’ skimmer. Pete snatched at the controls and we took off crooked down the street.

“Sorry folks, one of the anti-grav’s is busted, but it’ll get us there,” he announced.

Despite the awkward ride, we moved quickly out of town and into the open terrain, pockmarked by small craters both manmade and natural. Eventually, we rounded a curve near a rock outcropping and saw structures stickin’ up in the distance.

“Hang on!” Pete cautioned as he opened up the throttle. I felt my gut wanna leave my inners as we all hung on. We made it to an open-gated entrance in no time flat. This place was different lookin’ from the town. It was more modern, with square and circular shaped buildings attached to one another by above ground tunnels.

“Where’s the mine?” Sam asked.

“Down in the valley beyond us,” Pete quickly pointed. “I think that’s where they have their jump-ship. But, the wounded are all here, far as I know.”

Pete made a panic stop in front of one of the larger buildings. Then the roof of the skimmer slid back to let us all out.

"C'mon!" he shouted at us as he left the vehicle and trotted over to a set of doors. He placed a hand on a flat panel and the doors slid open.

"How do we know this ain't a trick, Wyatt?" Sam whispered to me as we trotted behind Pete.

"If it is, Pete gets it first," I replied.

"I heard that! This ain't no trick boys," Pete shouted over his shoulder, "there's been enough killin' this day to suit me the rest of my life. Over here!" he ordered, turning a corner, down a long hallway and then through another set of double-sliding doors. As soon as they slid open we could smell acrid fumes and there was dark smoke hangin' heavy in the air.

"We need to get whoever is wounded out of this room, quickly," Doc Adamson said.

Quinn was having trouble with his arm and motioned for Josie to go ahead and stay up with us. "I'll be fine," he said, trying to smile.

"Jack, wait in the hall and keep an eye out," she said. Quinn winked at her and pulled his gun.

The rest of us went inside. There had, indeed, been an explosion. Counters, furniture, parts of the ceiling and equipment were scattered all over the place. We came across the first body, but there wasn't much to save. The doc examined a few others, but shook his head in disappointment.

"Over here, Doc," Pete said from another part of the room.

We went over and found several people, both men and women, sprawled out on the floor, pretty banged up. The doctor went to work and Josie assisted as best she could. After a while of makeshift triage, splints, bandages, and several doses of strong Hypo-sprays to stabilize, we managed to drag or carry 'em out and carefully load them into the skimmer.

"Are there any more?" Doc Adamson asked Pete.

"Dunno, maybe," he replied, puffing for air.

"Well, alright," I said, gasping myself, "let's go look. Quinn, you stay with the skimmer. Guard the wounded and keep an eye out. It's fixin' to be dark soon," I said as we all looked at up at Mynos rising to cover the star.

"We can check some of the other rooms," Pete suggested.

"Did anyone see a ship take off?" Sam asked.

"I didn't, maybe some of the others might've," Pete replied.

"Where is everybody anyway?" Quinn asked.

"Prolly skedaddled every which-way after the explosion."

"Where's this ship?" I asked.

“Alright, there’s a tunnel with a shuttle leading down to the mine complex. We can start there,” Pete said.

“We look for wounded first,” Doc Adamson insisted.

“Fine, let’s go,” I said.

“What’re we supposed to do about these wounded anyway?” Josie asked.

“The supply transport isn’t due for a few more days,” Doc Adamson replied. “Them folks need to be taken to a proper medical facility planet side as soon as possible.”

“We already tried contactin’ the authority planet side, but somebody damaged the Com-System on this end,” Pete lamented.

“Oh, that’s just swell,” Josie replied. “Now what?”

“Looks like that outlaw jump-ship may be our only way off this rock,” Sam said.

“Well then, let’s go get it,” I said.

“Hang on,” Pete said, as he rummaged around in his pockets. He found and took out a small device and handed it to Quinn. “Keep this transmitter turned on and tuned to this frequency. We’ll let ya know if we find that ship. If we do, you think you can you drive this rig to where we’ll be?”

“Guess I’ll have-ta,” he grinned, then winced as he moved his wounded arm the wrong way.

“You keep yer eyes open, boy,” I ordered, jabbing a

finger at him.

“You got it, sir,” he replied, taking out his weapon and spinning it around his finger. I shook my head and walked away. Josie took the time to peck him on the cheek.

Leaving Quinn, the rest of us went back inside, through the shattered room and into more adjoining labs. We found another body. It looked like the victim had been neatly cleaved in half with a hot knife.

“Energy weapon, prolly a rifle,” Sam said, shaking his head and taking Josie by the arm. “Don’t look,” he said to her.

“C’mon, let’s keep movin’,” I said, spitting quickly and going forward.

“That’s probably what set off the explosion,” the doctor suggested. “Lasers and volatile gases don’t mix well.”

I pulled up short in the next room as we stopped and looked around in amazement. The whole place was lined with clear tanks filled with a yellow liquid, and inside them tanks were ...”

“God Almighty,” I gasped, “what kinda ..?”

Josie and Sam just stared in shock.

There were ... bodies, bodies of people, ...babies, then children, at various stages of growth ... but there was something strange about them.

“They were at the final stage of the duplication

process!" Doc Adamson said with a measure of scientific reverence. "This is unbelievable, I had no idea ...."

"This ain't right," Sam interjected. "C'mon, Wyatt, let's get outta here."

We pushed on, down corridors to other rooms and found ... more bodies. Bodies of both men and women, hairless, dressed in cloth jumpsuits, and each one pockmarked with neat, bloodless holes through their heads.

Josie screamed.

"What're they?" Sam asked.

Doc Adamson held his chest. "Clones, my boy," he said, solemnly, "fully formed .... I can't believe what I'm seeing ... I can't believe ..."

"And, they're dead," I said, grabbing him roughly and shaking. "Look, Doc, we can't help these poor souls, but we can help those wounded you patched up. So snap out of it and let's find that ship."

I pushed him forward, leaving the bodies where they lay.

"I gotta be dreamin' all this," Sam said as we hoofed it away from the grim scene behind us.

"Who would do such a thing?" Josie said.

"Well, we're gonna find out," I answered.

We finally made it to the tunnel connecting the lab complex to the ore mines, and waiting for us, on rails, was a small open shuttle.

“Hop in,” Sam said, getting into the front where the controls were. Once in, we took off into a black hole in the wall. After a few feet though, the ceiling of the tube we were in lit up with a row of lights. Sam pushed the throttle to the limit and the air rushed by our heads.

“How long till we’re there,” I asked Pete.

“Not long at this speed,” he replied.

The doctor sat next to me just staring forward, lost in thought. There were actually two sets of tracks, side by side, in the tunnel. A few minutes later we saw a light up ahead, on the opposite track, coming towards us.

“What’da ya think?” Sam asked, pointing up ahead.

“Pete?” I said.

Before he could answer, we saw a flash of bright light coming from the approaching shuttle and a second later a jagged line of molten metal appeared on the cowl of our vehicle.

“Heads down!” Sam yelled, grabbing Josie sitting next to him and pushing her down onto the floor. That’s when I took off my hat and stood up, Colt in hand. I drew a bead on the fast approaching head light and fired. It sounded like a cannon going off as the concussion echoed off the walls. The light went out and I could vaguely see heads bobbing. I cocked and fired again, this time seeing something resembling a man fall off the back of the car. Then another flash of heated light saturated the air between the two approaching shuttles. Josie jumped up and screamed as smoke boiled out from where she was. I figured she was hit, so I fanned the Colt empty and then started snatching bullets for a reload. Just then, Pete hollered out.

"It's slowin' down!"

Pete pulled the throttle back and put the air brakes on. He was right, the oncoming car was slowing down to a crawl. Sam pulled his weapon and got out as soon as our car stopped.

"Josie?" I hollered with concern, as I inserted the last shell into the Colt.

"I'm fine, daddy," she replied, slapping at a burning hole on her coat sleeve. "Go get 'em!" she ordered.

I didn't need the encouragement. I jumped out, weapon ready as Sam and I approached the now unmoving car.

"If anyone's alive in there don't move or you won't be for long!" Sam yelled at the vehicle. No one answered and there was no movement … at least until we got up close.

There were two men left in the car. One slouched over the controls in front and one behind with an odd looking rifle next to him on the seat. The driver was shot through the head, his open eyes tellin' us he was beyond help. The other, however, held his chest and was breathing heavily.

“Don’t shoot,” he said, “don’t ...”

“We ain’t gonna shoot ya,” Sam replied, taking the wounded man’s rifle by the strap and slinging it over a shoulder. I kept him covered, just in case.

“Any more comin’ behind ya?” I asked. The wounded man coughed up some blood and shook his head.

“No ... jus us ...” he rasped.

“Where’s Judas Long? Where’s his ship?” I pressed.

“Why should I say?” the man replied, starting to shake.

“Because you’re dyin’ and I’d advise ya to make yer peace before you go out,” I said, now holstering my gun. “Where’s Long and the ship?”

The man looked up with hollow eyes. “He’s back at the hangar loadin’ up to jump this rock,” he replied heavily.

“Where’s the hanger? In the mine?” Sam asked.

“Half-dome building ... behind the power plant, there’s sentries ... there’s ...” then his head dropped onto his chest. By this time Doc Adamson had come over, tried to find a pulse, but shook his head.

“C’mon, we just caught a break,” I said, as we headed back to our shuttle and took off again. “Tell Quinn to start headin’ down here,” I told Pete.

The mining buildings looked deserted, like a ghost town, when we got there. We were also greeted by a few more men, lying dead, from energy weapon fire. It was twilight outside and the thin air was getting colder. And, I was thankful we no longer needed to wear those infernal glasses to see. We quickly trotted, mindin' our footing, to the edge of a row of buildings. Sam peeked around the corner. Sure enough, there was a large, half-shell of a Dome off by itself. And inside the gaping entrance sat a ship, cargo bays open with men and BoTs loading cargo. Sam had an idea. He stepped back a few paces and then jumped, landing easily above us on the arched roof of the building we were crouched behind. After a few minutes he dropped back down to us.

"That dead fella was right, there's at least three sentries with rifles around that ship … and a man yellin' orders."

"Judas Long," I said.

"Maybe, I dunno. But, I also saw blond hair standin' next to him."

"That's gotta be that crazy bartender Flo," Josie said.

"Yeah, sure looked like her. Now what?" Sam said.

"Well," I began, "let's see. Pete do they know you 'round here?"

"Yep, I guess I'm a familiar face," he said.

"Well, we need a distraction so Sam, Josie and I can get in position and come at them from three directions. So, can ya walk in there and tell 'em that we've all been killed?"

"Yes, sir, I guess, but then what? That ain't gonna take much time to do," Pete replied.

"I can help," Doc Adamson suddenly volunteered.

"Doc, you're too valuable," I replied.

"Yes, please, Doctor, you need to stay behind," Josie insisted.

"I know him ... Judas Long. He's one of us," Adamson confessed.

"Huh? What'da ya mean he's 'one of you?'" Sam said.

Doc Adamson pinched the bridge of his nose momentarily and then took a deep breath.

"I mean he's a scientist, a researcher, like me. We worked together, on the ship ... during the crossing ...."

"The crossing?" Josie replied. "What? Doctor Adamson, that was hundreds of years ago, how can you say ...?"

"Oh, here we go again!" Sam blurted. "Look, Doc, we don't have time for this stuff right now ..."

"Hold up, Sam," I said. "That's not the point. Doc, you say you know Long? You tellin' us the truth?"

Adamson nodded. “I want some answers from him, about the work he’s done here ... about the future of our race here. I need to speak with him, Mr. Earp ... before you kill him.”

“I could tell Long he made me bring him here,” Pete said. “Maybe that’ll give you enough time to surround ‘em?”

“Daddy, I dunno about ...”

“Okay, Doc, it’s settled,” I cut Josie off. “You and Pete do a good job of keepin’ Long talkin’ while Sam, Josie and me get in position. Now, I just as soon they all surrender peacefully, but if they don’t, Pete, you and the Doc here need to keep yer heads down and find some cover. You got it?” I instructed.

They nodded, looked at each other, shook hands and then walked around the corner and towards the hanger. By this time, it was dark and the sky was a gauzy film of stars.

“Alright, Josie girl, I want you to stay low and cut around to that side,” I gestured and pointed my instructions to her.

“Here,” Sam said, unslinging the rifle, “take this and cover us from a distance. It’s got pretty good range, just mind your eyes.”

“I know, Sam,” she replied with a grin.

“You do?” I said.

“Yes, daddy, you taught me to shoot before I was potty trained.”

“I did?”

“Don’t worry, I got your backs,” she replied, confidently. Then she kissed me briefly on the cheek and took off into the darkness.

“She’s all you, Wyatt,” Sam said. “Now, what about us?”

“Sam, you seem to like to jump. Why don’t you see if you can get behind ‘em,” I suggested.

“Alright, what’re you gonna do?”

“I intend to walk right up and tell ‘em to surrender,” I replied, reaching into a pocket and pullin’ out an old fashioned metal Marshal’s Star which I pinned onto the outside of my duster.

“Where’d ya get that antique?” Sam squinted.

“Josie slipped it to me when ya’ll came to break me outta the hospital. I remember this,” I said, touching the star. “It was my great granddaddy’s, handed down from his.”

“Your memory comin’ back is it, Wyatt?”

“No. But, I remember this. Now, get goin’, them two greenhorns don’t have much time, I suspect.”

Sam and I shook hands and then he stood back and leaped up onto the roof like a big jack rabbit.

I moved to the edge of the corner and peeked around. Sure enough, I could just make out Pete and Doc Adamson talkin’ to a small circle of men in the dim lights of the hanger and the ship. I waited as long as I figured it would take Sam and Josie to get in position. Then I stood tall, checked my gun, adjusted my hat and stepped around the corner.

~6~

"Please understand," Doctor Adamson said to the tall man in the center of the little group that surrounded them. Some held hand weapons trained on the newcomers. "I just want to be a part of this grand research. I've seen the results. You've done it, haven't you? You've overcome our reproductive problem by the use of clones … I have so many questions, David, please let me …."

"Don't call me that! I no longer go by that name, haven't for a long time, Lawrence … or is it 'Doc' now? I understand the town folk call you that. How quaint, but a considerable demotion from what you were back on board the ARK or in SouthDOME," the tall man replied.

"And how did a brilliant scientist become Judas Long? A thief, a robber … and a murderer, from what I understand," Doc Adamson said.

“Because circumstances warranted it!” Long snapped back. “You don’t remember? We brought the bureaucrats and the lawyers with us from Terra. Why? We should’ve spaced ‘em all when we left Terran orbit. Nothing changed on the voyage here. We were supposed to have a new start on a new world, a new frontier. We brought with us the most enlightened men and women of science we had. But, *they* wanted to curtail, stifle and compartmentalize everything we purposed for the future. They wanted complete control so that we would have the same disastrous results we had back home on Terra. I, along with some others, *and you*, foresaw what was coming as soon as we emerged from STASIS. So, I did something about it. I acted before they did and I’m not sorry for it.”

“But, I understand you’re negotiating for peace, aren’t you, with the Colonial Government, to end this impasse?” Doc Adamson replied.

They all broke out laughing as the doctor and Pete looked nervously at each other.

“You’re so naive, Lawrence, you always were. You have no vision.” Long chuckled.

“Judas, why don’t you let me burn these two into ash and let’s finish loading and get outta here,” Flo said, raising her weapon.

Long raised a hand in caution. “You should have stayed with us Lawrence instead of siding with *them.* You have no idea how far we’ve come, how far beyond what the government’s suppressed research has accomplished.”

“Yes, I do! I’ve seen the tanks, the bodies ... by the way, why did you kill them?”

“They were blanks, cut-outs, stencils, test patterns. They’ve served their purpose and we have no room to take them with us when we leave ... which reminds me. Flo, didn’t I specifically say no bodies left behind. I wanted complete disintegration of any evidence.”

“I’ll see to it as soon as we take care of these two,” she replied with a smile. “And you say that use-to-be Marshal and his friends are dead?” she asked, looking at Pete.

“Uh, yes, ma’am ... I done saw the bodies,” Pete lied nervously.

“Well, see to it that they’re vaporized, as well as the rest of the staff that thought they could double-cross me,” Long ordered.

“Sure thing,” Flo replied.

“Was that the cause of the explosion in the lab?” Adamson asked.

“Yes, Lawrence, a slight rebellion of some of my loyal supporters. But, it’s over now for them.”

“What about the project? Tell me what you’ve done to help our species here?”

Suddenly, there was a voice from behind everyone.

“Alright! Nobody moves and nobody else dies! You’re all under arrest by order of the Marshal’s office!" I said loudly.

Both Pete and the doctor took off at a dead run for the ship.

"Kill 'em!" Flo hollered to the guards standing around.

Before the startled guards could fire, several flashes of red hit them dead center in the torso and they went down clutching their smoldering chests.

Flo raised her weapon to shoot. I drew and fired. The Colt barked, a jet of flame shooting out of the barrel, and Flo dropped to her knees, a neat round hole now decorating her forehead.

"Flo!" Long screamed.

"Judas Long, my name is Wyatt Earp, and I'm here to take you in, dead or alive ... your choice!" I said, walking quickly forward, as several more sentries fell to the ground as Sam cut loose from behind.

"We're wasting human lives!" I yelled to the rest. "Don't be stupid, there's no future for us if we kill each other! Surrender in the name of the Law!"

The rest of the men scattered like rabbits, dropping weapons as they fled.

Judas Long screamed in rage, cursed, then turned and ran, bounding toward his ship.

I leveled my weapon at him and cocked the hammer back. I had a perfect shot.

“Would great granddaddy back-shoot a fella?” Josie’s voice said from behind me.

“That’s not the Wyatt Earp I wanna serve with,” Sam said, walking up to join us.

I sighed and uncocked the hammer. “Since when did you two become my conscience,” I said, looking at them both. They didn’t reply. “Thanks,” I said.

“Then let’s finish this,” Sam said

“Yeah, let’s go get ‘em,” Josie agreed. And, we did.

Sam expertly covered the distance and was inside the ship before we were. We quickly joined him and began the search, drawing our weapons at crew members who really had no stomach for a fight. I told ‘em to get lost and they did without incident. However, I grabbed one fella by the arm.

“Tell us where Judas Long went or else,” I threatened.

He pointed aft and I turned him loose.

“C’mon, watch your heads,” I said.

The ship we were on, I learned later, was a standard Colonial Cub-Class freighter, modified with a jump drive for a fast getaway. The passageways were narrow and the ceilings low as we made our way into the bowels of the thing. We rounded a corner and saw someone. It looked like a young man wearing a pair of ship grey coveralls. I shouted at him. “Hey! Don’t move or I’ll shoot!” I said. The man froze in place and put his hands up. We all approached. “Alright, turn around," I said. He did … and when he did …

"Jack!" Josie said in surprise, "how'd you get on board?"

Jack Quinn looked at Josie and then at all of us in turn, but didn't seem to act like he recognized any of us.

"I'm sorry," he apologized; his diction was punctuated and very precise, "but I don't know a Jack. Whom are you looking for?"

"That ain't Quinn," I said, "look at his eyes."

The young man's eyes were large, but not overly so, and they were bright amber in color.

"Good lord, they've duplicated Quinn," Josie breathed in amazement.

"I'm sorry, but I do not know a Quinn either," the young man replied, smiling.

"Where's Judas Long?" I asked.

"Oh, that I can assist you with. He just passed me in this corridor a few minutes ago."

"Where would he go?" Josie asked.

"I would imagine to the quarters, where the others are."

"What others?" Sam asked.

"Why, like me."

"Let's go," I said.

“Wait, what’s your name?” Josie asked as we moved away.

“Number three,” he replied with a pleasant smile.

We hurried off in the direction the young man had pointed and we soon came to a round room with several, dark passageways leading in other directions.

“Now what?” Sam said, walking to the center. Then lightning struck, propelling him backwards into a bulkhead.

“Sam!” Josie screamed.

“Josie, get down!” I yelled as another bolt crackled through the air.

“Leave now, Marshal,” a voice, seeming to come from everywhere, said.

“You’re comin’ with me, one way or another,” I yelled.

“Fool, you have no idea what you’re doing or who you’re dealing with. I’ll spare you and the girl if you leave my ship now!” the voice boomed.

“Sam,” Josie called, looking over at his crumpled body lying a few feet away.

“I’m bringing you in for the murder of Josephine Earp and Sam Holland, who you just cut down!”

“Your man isn’t dead, just stunned for now. And, as far as this woman, it was self-defense, she fired first, I had no choice at the time.”

“There’s always a choice!” I yelled with contempt, “I coulda back shot you outside, I won’t make the same mistake again. Now, come on out or no mercy!”

Again, the air crackled with several streaks of intense light as Josie and I hugged the deck.

“Those beams he’s usin’ now won’t stun if we’re hit,” Josie said, looking up briefly.

“Do ya see where they’re comin’ from?” I said.

Another round of fire erupted, pockmarking the walls and filling the air with the smell of burning metal.

“There,” Josie pointed, “to the left, that passageway … I think.”

“You think?” I said, and then sighed. “Alright, get ready.”

“Daddy, what’re ya gonna do?” she said as she checked her weapon.

“Ready?” I said.

“Daddy!”

I jumped up, rolled to the middle of the room and fired point blank down the hall and kept firing until my gun just clicked on spent bullets. After a few seconds, I saw a figure runnin’ towards me and then a streak of bright red light. The light hit my Colt and the barrel melted away as I dropped it. Judas Long now appeared in the room and saw that he’d missed me. He raised his weapon and fired … or someone did.

Judas Long stood there momentarily in amazement as he looked down at the growing circle of red in the middle of his chest. He dropped his weapon and stumbled backward into the wall, then slid down it to the floor. Josie sat on her haunches, both arms outstretched, holding her smoldering gun clutched tightly in her hands.

"That's for you, momma," she whispered, as if in prayer.

I went over and knelt down beside him. He gurgled something.

"It didn't have to end this way," I said.

"Yes ... it did," he coughed. "Tell Lawrence to use my research ... save us from extinction in this place. Tell him it's all on the ships computer. Tell him, I'm sorry ...."

"Yeah, I'll tell 'em alright," I said as Josie now joined me.

Long looked up at her and smiled slightly, a small trickle of blood now running out of the corner of his mouth.

"I'm sorry about ..." he said to her, "you look a lot like her. I tried to make it right ... make it right for both of you ... for all our sakes ..." he looked up at me and chuckled slightly. "Wyatt Earp ... how profound ...."

Judas Long exhaled his final breath. His eyes set and stared up at me. I looked back into them for what seemed like a long time, tryin' to remember the hate I knew I must have had for the man, but now was empty.

"Daddy," I heard Josie say. I snapped out of it and stood up. That's when Sam came to, cursing like a drunk.

"What hit me?" he spat, climbing up on his hands and knees.

"Pulse Stunner," Josie replied. "Just be thankful it wasn't what fried daddy's Colt.

I had gone over and picked up what was left of my Colt Model 1873 'Peacemaker' ... it was a lost cause.

"You'll make a new one," Josie said.

Sam stood up, wobbled, held his head, and then came over and stood next to Josie. They both looked down at the body of Judas Long.

"You alright, girl?" he said.

"Yeah," Josie simply replied. "Let's get Quinn and those wounded folks and get off this rock."

"Hang on," I said, "we're not alone," I pointed down the passageway where Long was hiding and I could see ... movement.

"Who's down there?" Sam called.

"It's us," a familiar voice replied. "It's Pete, and the Doc is here too. You need to come see this."

Sam, Josie and I walked down to where Pete stood before an open steel door to another room.

“In there,” he pointed with a thumb. We walked in and saw Doc Adamson speaking with, and examining a dozen or more men and women dressed in the same ship-grey overalls as the Quinn lookalike we met earlier ... or did we? Because I laid my eyes on two more Jack Quinns in the room.

“Jack ...” Josie whispered. And, there were others, twins and triplets, who were identical right down to their amber eyes.

“Marshal Earp,” Doc Adamson said as he turned around. “What of Lawrence, I mean, Judas Long?”

I shook my head and he understood.

“He said he left all the research for you in the ships computer,” Josie said.

The doctor nodded, sighed and then gestured to the others in the room. “These are the products of years of research,” he stated proudly. “A perfect amalgam of human and Menutan genomes.”

“Clones?” I replied.

“Clones indeed,” Doc Adamson said.

“How’re they gonna help us?” Sam asked.

The doctor smiled, “You’ll see and understand in time,” he said. “Oh, and there’s something else. Come, come see,” he beckoned to Josie and me. “Here, in this other room. Come.”

The doctor led the way into another adjoining room. In the center stood a lone, dark haired woman, with her back towards us as we entered.

"Ma'am," Doc Adamson quietly said, "you have visitors." And then, he turned and left.

The woman wore a simple long garment that reached to the floor.

"Ma'am, can we help you?" I asked.

The woman turned slowly around to face us. Josie gasped, putting her hands over her mouth as if she'd seen a ghost.

"Momma? Momma, is that you?" she asked the woman.

"Momma?" I replied, "Josie, what're you sayin'? Do you know this woman?"

"Oh my God! Daddy, it's momma ... your wife!" she replied. Then she ran over and embraced the woman around the middle and wept.

The woman, at first, had a look of surprise on her face, but then she slowly stroked Josie's hair and began to speak consolingly to her. She finally took Josie's face in both her hands and studied her. Josie looked up into the woman's amber eyes.

"Dear child," the woman began softly, "I see myself in your face. So, there must be some of you in me, and me in you. I hope we can become friends."

"Yes, yes," Josie sobbed, holding her hands, "I'd

like that very much.”

“Josie?” was all I could say.

“Daddy, come meet Josephine ... oh, I’m sorry, what *is* your name?” Josie apologized.

“Josephine is a beautiful name. That will do,” she replied. Her smile was bright.

I removed my hat and walked over. The woman, Josephine, extended her hand to me and I took it.

“It’s a pleasure to meet you, sir,” she said cordially.

“It’s Wyatt, Wyatt Earp,” I said, something catching in my throat.

“Wyatt ...” she repeated several times as she closed her eyes. “Strange, I seem to remember that name for some reason, like an echo of a distant memory. Perhaps I’m malfunctioning and need a scan?” she said, looking at me again.

“No, ma’am,” I said. “I’m thinkin’ you’re right as rain.”

~7~

The following several weeks were both unsettling and historic, depending on who you were talkin' to. Quinn made it to the jump-ship with the wounded and, after locating a pilot, we all landed safely at NorthDOME, Adelaide City, where we were greeted by a small army of security who quickly arrested everyone on board the ship, especially Sam, Josie and myself. We were questioned for hours that yielded little results as far as clearing things up. Finally, someone in the government who had authority and some common sense formed a panel and invited Dr. Adamson, Sam, Josie, me, Dr. Xhin and a few others to explain from the beginning the details of what happened here and on the moon, *Paulo Mynos.* The panel listened patiently for several hours of testimony and then adjourned to discuss things. What was disturbing Josie, Sam and I the most was what happened to our passengers on board the jump-ship, especially to Josephine.

As it turned out, we were all exonerated, the charges dropped against me, and my Marshal's status returned. We asked about the clones and were told they were safe and that we were to keep their existence a state secret until further notice. They made us all swear an oath and then they provided transport for the long trip back to South Dome and then home on the Rim.

Well, more time passed, months actually. I received treatments for my damaged lungs and innards, which have since grown back to normal just fine. I have also been examined several times more by 'experts' with regard to my memory loss, but no one could give me a straight answer as to when or *if* my full memory will ever return ... which was fine and dandy, according to most folks who knew me. They seem to enjoy the new me more so than the old. However, I had to relearn all my duties back at the SouthRIM District Law Enforcement Office Complex, South West Territory. Everyone seemed friendly and considerate and once I got the hang of it I was, once again, keeping the peace. Not that there were any outlaws to deal with anymore. Most folks were too concerned about getting along now for the sake of the human race and its survival on this world.

During this time, several 'official' and lengthy announcements were broadcasted planet wide over the Vid-Screens. It seems there had been some major medical and scientific breakthroughs with regard to our declining birth rate and the need for the general population to be reeducated with regard to genetics ... ours and the Menutans. It really wasn't debatable any longer; it was a matter of going with the science or ceasing to exist as a race within a few short decades. While there was some grumbling, old prejudices were quickly thrust aside for a more enlightened New World philosophy.

And so it began ... the inoculations. A series of them designed to change our gene pool forever in order to survive in this star system. There would be no more ARK ships built. The originals were scuttled long ago for the raw materials. This was it. Terra Mynos 1 was humanity's home from now on in this part of the galaxy.

It was heartwarming to see Dr. Adamson leading the research team on this new adventure ... 'a brave new world' he called it during a brief visit to us one day. He explained that Doctor Lawrence "Judas" Long had figured out a way to change our genes with Menutan chromosomes just enough so that children born would still be human, but with the ability to now reproduce normally in this environment. Some things would be a little different though, he explained. Human gestation would now be around fourteen months, instead of the usual nine (which was a sight better than the Native three year pregnancy) and, most of the children born would have amber eyes. As far as the clones we encountered from the ship, being the products of the early research, they were both fully human *and* fully Menutan, but sterile. They desired to settle in amongst the people and live out their lives ... and that was granted.

Doc Adamson did not come alone when he visited. He brought along Pete and his wife, who was pregnant for the first time in her long life ... and Quinn, who proposed to Josie in front of everyone after dinner one evening. She accepted and my feet itched. They also brought Josephine with them, and we spent considerable time acquainting her with her genetic founder. Josie and Josephine seemed to quickly become fast friends. It was even more of a surprise when she asked to stay on with us.

That seems like some time ago now. Josie and Quinn are married and she's expecting. Sam and his wife are not far behind. As for me, I enjoy walking outside on a starry night (and yes, I'm able now to be outdoors without that blasted respirator) looking up at the billions of stars that make up our existence. I stand out here often lost in thought ... until I feel a warm hand take my arm. I look over at Josephine, who smiles back at me. We stand, side by side and look heavenward while we talk and plan our lives together.

I used to be a man lost and wounded. A man in a desert. Now, I know who I am.

Brenton Udor

Freak on a School Bus

I really liked Gary Lewis and the Playboys, Herman's Hermits, Paul Revere (not the American hero) and the Raiders and, yes, John, Paul, George and Ringo, affectionately called: The Beatles. In fact, every chance I got I had my head glued to the radio we had in the kitchen and dialed to the A.M. station that played the latest tunes on the Hit Parade. The radio was also an invaluable resource with regard to whether or not there was going to be school that day, as winter storms coming off of the Great Lakes in blizzard form would, most frequently, close down the entire school system, some seasons for weeks at a time (and I smiled in approval when that happened).

As I look back, I don't think school ever really liked me. I tried my best to cooperate with the whole arrangement, as nonsensical as it seemed. It wasn't actually the class work that was that difficult either, although I really had a hard time with math and still do to this day. The problem(s) centered more on the 'social interaction' with and among the other students (or convicts depending on who we're talking about).

I was a 'farm kid,' having been raised in the rurals. Therefore, I went to a small town school with a graduating class of a whopping seventy. Yes, it was my personal microcosm ...my little universe that I would be transported to five days a week (weather permitting) during the course of my twelve year sentence. Being raised in the country (and alone) gave me ample opportunity, especially during summer recess, to indulge in and exercise my vivid imagination, especially when it came to the genre of science fiction with all the wonder that it generated. Why, I saw aliens everywhere: in the cellar, the woods, barn, closet, under my bed, etc ... and especially, in myself (I would really have preferred *not* to have been 'of this world' during this period of my life). I was simply one of those kids who would perch himself on a tree limb and wile away a summer's day dreaming of fantastic places, races and landscapes. My mind was fertile ground for the likes of Robert Heinlein, Isaac Asimov and Marvel Comics (which I devoured religiously) as well as the popular T.V. shows of the period. However, September came all too soon, and with it, the realities of yet another seemingly endless school year, and along with that the terrors of ...the school bus.

"If I can just find a seat towards the front," I whispered to myself in a prayerful litany as I waited at the end of our endlessly long driveway for that yellow monster that would soon devour me yet again. I could hear the roar of the thing as it stopped to scoop up one of the neighbor kids down the dirt road. My house seemed so far away from where I stood, too far to run back and feign a stomachache to my mother who would sometimes look out the window to make sure I was gobbled-up without incident. I considered myself the adolescent 'Prince of Sickness,' a student hypochondriac who would visit the nurse's office so frequently that the woman practically had a bed set aside for me with my name on a 3x5 above it.

My mother, however, was less tolerant and would shake her head and finger, point me towards the door and the harsh reality that lay beyond the safety of my bedroom. Ah, yes, my bedroom! A second floor sanctuary I shared with an imaginary brother across the hallway from my parents' room where my father snored like thunder through most nights ... unless, of course, there was an actual thunder storm outside that rattled the window sills and caused me to bury myself, like a hamster, in a pile of bed sheets and blankets. Even on the hottest summer nights without air conditioning (what was that?) I always covered myself with a 'force field' consisting physically of a sheet and at least one light blanket. Of course, every kid knows that no monster, evil spirit or probing alien visitor can get past such a mighty and impenetrable barrier. I would spend endless hours locked in my room ... my womb, huddled over a register (a hot air heating vent in the wood floor) next to my desk, surrounded by a blanket on many a cold winter night and dream wondrous fantasies about how things could be, should be ... about the future, that was as much of a mystery to me as the starry skies I would get lost in outside ... or girls. Speaking of which, there were several over the period of my adolescent insanity who totally, unmercifully, and, for the most part, unknowingly, ground my already fractured heart into a quivering jelly of unfulfilled expectations and my face into raging outbreaks of acne. My defense from all this? My solitude, my daydreams, my vivid imagination ... and, of course, my friend ,Willis.

He came to me one day after a particularly harrowing bus ride home. The thugs who inhabited the yellow monster like intestinal parasites relished the time they could spend making my life a veritable 'living hell.' Later that evening, after supper, I went for a walk to one of my favorite haunts, a wooded hillside with a gravel pit where all was sane, peaceful and quiet. A place where I could breathe and wear out my homemade 'Davidic' sling, sending rocks crashing through the trees and underbrush as I slew imaginary dragons, and not so few, fellow classmates. I recall squatting down to find another smooth rock to launch when, suddenly, a pair of odd feet came into view. They were 'odd' to me because they had no toes. I jumped up shouting expletives at the creature that now stood before me. I'll describe him this way: He (I think) was my size, same build, with a rather large head .... Well, his forehead actually seemed to protrude somewhat past his eyebrow (one eyebrow) and the rest of his head was covered with fine, short, dark hair. He had a thin nose and lips, and long fingers (three on each hand, plus a thumb). I think what wigged me out the most was he was the most disturbing shade of green. Not that he, or it, was naked. He wore a silver, iridescent body suit of some kind, but no shoes.

We stood there and looked at each other for who knows how long. My first rational thoughts were that I was home in bed dreaming ... followed by I was dead and had gone to hell ... followed by, 'I've finally lost my mind' ... followed by 'this is some kinda queer joke being played on me' ... followed by, 'this isn't October 31st, is it'? Then he/it spoke.

"I assure you, you are not dreaming, crazy, dead or being made a fool of ... and what is the significance of October 31?"

He spoke very good English for a ...

"What're you? Who're you? Where'd you come from? Why're you here? What'da ya want with me? I wanna go home ...." I blurted so fast that the green guy's eyes, which, by the way, were large and without pupils, squinted as if he was trying to comprehend what I'd said.

"Which question should I answer first?" he finally asked.

"Oh God!" I exclaimed. "I'm gonna puke."

"No, I am not a deity. Do you require one?" he said calmly. "By the way, what is puke?"

I showed him. He seemed to study it, then turned up his nose at the smell.

"Perhaps it would be beneficial if you sat down?" he suggested.

It was starting to get dark and I could see the porch light go on at the house which was a signal for me to be inside or get hollered at.

“Look, I gotta go,” I said, stepping backward slowly.

“Go? Where?” he said.

“Uh, home ... you know, home, where I live. Shouldn’t you go home now? Yeah, that’s a great idea, you should go home too,” I stuttered as I continued to move further away.

“That is impossible for the time being,” he replied. Then he began to walk towards me. “May I accompany you to your home?”

“No! I mean ...look, my mom and dad would call the sheriff or get the gun, or ... look, I can’t just bring you into my house with you lookin’ like ... and besides, how do I know you’re not ... dangerous!”

“I understand,” he said. “I assure you, I am not dangerous and your mom and dad, whatever they are, will not detect my presence.”

“Huh?”

“That is to say, I am invisible to others of your kind, except to you,” he smiled.

“Huh? How’s that possible? Unless I’m nuts or ...”

“I assure you that you are sentient and in full control of your mental faculties. I have been observing you since my arrival here and have chosen to reveal myself to you, and only to you, for the duration of my stay. I assure you that I mean you no harm, but I do require shelter and sustenance to survive. Is it possible for you to provide this?"

I guess I musta passed out, because when I woke up he was looking down at me and touching my face with one of his long fingers.

"Excuse me, but someone is calling you I believe," he said.

"*Daniel! Daniel, come home now!*"

"Yipes, that's my mom! I'm in trouble," I said, jumping up, dusting off my britches and feeling the extra lump on the back of my head.

"Look, uhhh, Mister, I really gotta go. See ya," I said, and then I turned and ran as fast as my legs would carry me, back to my house, onto the porch, kicked off my sneakers, went inside, got chewed out by my parents, grabbed several cookies and headed to my room. I sat at my desk and looked into the small mirror that hung on the wall. I stared at myself and tried to make sense of what I saw at that gravel bed.

"Alright, look, Danny-boy, you fell and hit your head, had a bad dream, woke up, came home and now it's over," I said to the image. It smiled back and seemed satisfied to gnaw on a cookie ... that is until it was joined by the green guy. Again, more expletives leaped from my mouth as I jumped and turned around.

"Greetings! Daniel is it?" he said.

"How in the ...?"

“I apologize. I followed you to this dwelling. I did not relish spending the night outside, you have small flying creatures that bite and ...”

“Insects,” I replied. “Bugs, mosquitoes and other stuff in the woods,” I said, backing up to my bed and then sitting down. He picked up one of the cookies on my desk and sniffed at it.

“Sustenance?” he asked.

“Go ahead,” I said.

He seemed to study it for a few more seconds, after which he put it into his mouth, took a small bite, chewed carefully and then swallowed. After that, he gulped the rest down and smiled.

“Very stimulating,” he replied. “I think my vision has improved, although I am experiencing a dull pain in my cranium for some reason.”

“It’s prolly the sugar,” I said. “It’ll pass ... does me.”

“Sugar?”

“It’s sweet. We put it in food.”

“Why?”

“Makes us happy I guess. Gives ya energy too, well, at least it does me.”

“Sugar, I deduce, is a complex source of high energy output and possible propulsion, concentrated into an easily portable form for immediate assimilation and is also biologically stable enough for consumption. Is there more?” he rattled off.

"Uh, yeah, downstairs," I said.

"Would you mind?"

I rubbed my face, ran a hand through my hair and then went down past my parents who were engrossed in Lawrence Welk, grabbed a few more cookies and went back up. Mr. 'Green' was eager to wolf down a few more while I sat on my bed and stared at him.

"You gotta name?" I finally asked.

"You mean a designation, like 'Daniel'?" he replied.

"Yeah."

"Of course, it is ..."

And then he rattled off a string of gibberish that made my ears hurt.

"Don't ya have a nickname? Somethin' short I can call you by?" I asked.

His forehead wrinkled and he shook his head. Then he smiled.

"Why don't you give me a nickname?" he said.

"Oh swell ..." I remarked, rubbing my head. While I was doing so, he went over and looked at my bookshelf which consisted mostly of sci-fi classics.

"You also enjoy space travel?" he asked, looking closely at the row of paperbacks.

"Yes, well, only in stories. I haven't really gone anywhere," I replied.

“Do you have a favorite?” he asked, pointing at the row of books.

“Probably Red Planet. I’ve read it the most.”

He looked for it, found it, pulled it out and examined the cover.

“You can read English?” I asked.

“Yes, I have learned many of your languages. What is this?” he said, pointing to the cover illustration.

“Oh, that’s a picture of the main character’s pet, Willis. He’s a Martian roundhead, a bouncer … somethin’ like that,” I replied.

“Willis? Willis …can you call me that?”

I thought about it. “Yeah, sure, I suppose,” I replied with surprise.

“Agreed then. I will call you Daniel and you will call me Willis.” He smiled.

“How long did you say you were stayin’?” I asked.

“As long as it takes,” Willis replied, coming over and sitting next to me on the bed.

“Uh, as long as it takes for what?”

“For them to find me.”

“Them?”

“My companions.”

“There’s more of you?” my voice cracked.

"Yes. We became separated in transport, but they will locate me in time."

"Oh, I see (I didn't really). So, uh, Willis, where're you from anyway?"

"Not Mars," he smiled.

"Where then?"

"A place you have never heard of. One that your science will not discover for some time."

"Uh-huh, so you're from outer space?"

Willis laughed, at least I think it was a laugh, he was smiling when he made the noise.

"Your particular species seems to be infatuated with what is beyond your atmosphere. You have aspirations of traveling to other worlds. You spend a great deal of time thinking about what's up there (he pointed at the ceiling) rather than concentrating on what you have here in this place," he said, waving a hand around. "Why is that, Daniel?"

I yawned and tried to think of a cool answer. "I dunno. I guess it's because we're bored with earth."

"Bored?" he replied with surprise, "how can you become bored with a place so wonderful and full of life? The void of space is boring. Even your moon is boring, but yet you hurry to get there and once you do, then what? It makes no logical sense to me. You have so much to discover here on this world."

"I guess I never thought about it that way before," I replied.

"Did you know that your world is the most frequently visited planet by other life forms than any other place in the entire galaxy?"

"Well, no, I guess I didn't. What's so special about here?"

"Everything!" he beamed.

"Is that why you're here?"

"Yes, in a way."

"So you're an explorer?"

"Yes."

"You've obviously been here before."

"Yes, many times."

"Have you stayed with other people, like you are with me?"

"No, you are the first. This is an exceptional circumstance. I hope not to be an inconvenience for long."

"Oh, that's okay. So far it's been kinda cool," I said.

"You are cold? Your body temperature seems normal to me."

"Oh, no, what I mean by 'cool' is that I'm having a good time talkin' to you."

Willis smiled. “I’m glad you are not afraid.”

“Well, so far. Say, you don’t turn into something weird after midnight and need to eat human flesh do ya?”

Willis grew a disgusted look on his face.

“Uh, never mind,” I said, “just ignore that one. Say, look, I got school tomorrow so I need to hit the sack. I gotta sleeping bag in the closet. I can throw it on the floor over there and ...”

“Daniel, that won’t be necessary. I do not need to hit a sack or a bag. I will stand still against that wall until your star rises, will that be suitable?”

“You don’t sleep?” I asked.

“We have no need of experiencing unconsciousness as your species does. However, we do perform intercerebral maintenance which takes several hours based on your planet’s rotation. I also have a great deal of data to process which I have been neglecting. I will most probably be finished by the time you regain consciousness from your sack.

“Okay, a simple no would’ve been fine. Well, I need to use the can downstairs and then I’ll be back to, uh, hit my sack ... excuse me,” I said as I got up and headed for the door, then hesitated. “Willis, you said that only *I* can see you?”

“That is correct.”

“How’s that work?”

“I will explain when you recover in the morning. How will that be?”

“Cool, I mean fine ... great ...” I replied as I left and walked downstairs to wash up and take care of business. By the time I got back Willis was standing against the far wall, stiff as a board, and staring straight ahead. That was creepy enough. What really freaked me out was the bulge in his forehead ... it was movin’, kinda like a heartbeat. I turned away, started to take my clothes off, thought better of it and decided just to crawl into bed with my tee-shirt and jeans on. I also decided to leave the light on my nightstand on. I grabbed a handful of blankets and pulled them up over my head, but molded a small arch in them to breathe fresh air ... and to watch Willis, which I did for as long as I could, until the alarm clock shook me awake at 6:00 a.m. the next morning.

My eyelids snapped open. I was on my back and twisted up in the bedding, but I could move my head enough to look sideways and when I did I saw ... nothing! Just the bare wall across from me. I sat up and looked around the room. I was alone.

“What the...?” I said out loud, then wrestled myself outta the covers. I sat on the edge of my bed in my skivvies and began to rub my head. Then I remembered ... I got into bed last night with my jeans on ... and now ...

“Ahhh!” I squealed, fearing the worst.

“Daniel? Is there something wrong?” a voice said.

I made a complete three-sixty, but saw nothing ...

then I saw Willis walk through the wall and stand in the middle of the room.

"What happened?" I said to him.

"Happened? I don't understand?" Willis replied.

"Where'd you go to? How did you do that? Where's my pants? How did you ...?"

Willis held up a hand, palm out. "Which question shall I answer first?

"All of 'em," I said. "Did you probe me?"

"Probe you?" Willis replied, wrinkling his forehead.

"Yeah, you know, what aliens do to people ... you know."

"Oh!" Willis said and then he made that laughing noise. "Daniel, I'm afraid you have been reading too many books about 'aliens' written by other humans," he clucked. "And no, I most certainly did not probe you. We are very familiar with the human anatomy."

"Well then, how come my pants are off!"

"You seemed uncomfortable and your body temperature was unusually high, so I removed your trousers so you could breathe easier."

"Huh?" I said. "So, how'd you get 'em off me anyway?"

"Why, I dissolved them," Willis said, innocently.

"Dissolved 'em? What am I supposed to wear to school?"

"You do not possess others?"

"Well, yeah, but ... what am I suppose to tell my mother?"

"The trousers are hers?"

"No! But she buys 'em and does the laundry, she'll know they're missing."

"I see," Willis replied thoughtfully, rubbing his chin. "I suppose the logical thing to do is re-constitute them. I will do that during the course of this day."

"Re-what?"

"Never mind, just leave it to me."

"Yeah, whatever ..." I said, unconvinced as my stomach growled in protest.

"Are you ill?"

"Nah, hungry. I gotta get breakfast and then wait for the bus."

"The bus? What is 'the bus?'"

"It's a vehicle that picks me up and takes me to school."

"School? I know this term," Willis said. "You are being educated, correct?"

“Oh, yeah, if you say so,” I replied, digging out another pair of jeans from a drawer and then grabbing a shirt.

“You do not sound excited about expanding your mind.”

“I’m a kid, what can I say? Look, I gotta get goin’, Willis, why don’t you just make yourself at home until I get back later this afternoon, okay? Just don’t let my mom see ya, she’ll have-a fit.”

“As I have already explained, only you can see me.”

“Well, I sure didn’t when I woke up. Where’d you go anyway?”

“Oh, I transferred into an altered state for maintenance. I hope my absence didn’t disturb you?”

“Oh, no, I’m used to having little green men come walking through my wall when I first wake up.”

“You consider me little and green?”

“Well, no, it’s a figure of speech .... Look, Willis, I gotta take off or I’m gonna be late.” I hurried to finish getting dressed, then grabbed my coat and books.

“Take off? Does this bus vehicle you speak of have anti-gravitational properties?”

“Wha ... huh? No! Look, just stay here, I’ll be home around 3:00 or so, okay?”

“As you wish,” Willis replied.

“I ran down the stairs, wolfed down a bowl of cereal

in the kitchen and then headed out the door and down the driveway. About halfway to the road I heard something behind me. I turned and saw Willis following me, bare feet and all.

"Willis, what're you doin'?"

"I've decided to accompany you on your educational journey!" he said pleasantly.

"Oh, wait, hold on, you can't go with me to school," I protested.

"Is there a charge?"

"No! That's not the point. How am I gonna explain …?"

Willis furrowed his one eyebrow.

"Oh, yeah, that's right, only I can see you. Swell, they're gonna not only think I'm a freak, but nuts too," I lamented.

"A freak?" Willis repeated and we walked side by side. "What is freak?"

"You know, a freak, a weirdo, a nerd, not cool, a low-life, a …"

Willis held up a hand. "I'm sorry, Daniel, but these are terms I am not familiar with. Please explain."

" *I'm* a freak," I sighed. "Alright, look, I'm different. I'm not like the other kids. I'm treated different … I feel different …"

"How so?"

"Well, it's hard to explain, it's just that ... never mind, here it comes."

Sure enough, I could hear the roar of the diesel motor in the distance and soon a yellow bus came lumbering down the road at us.

"That is the bus? That is our transportation?"

"Yep," was all I said as the bus stopped right next to us and the door folded open.

"Morning," the driver barely said, as Willis and I climbed the three steps up into the monster's belly.

"Please let there be a seat close to the front," I whispered to myself as I negotiated my way down the narrow aisle towards the back. The bus was full as usual, mostly three to a seat as I squeezed my way towards the back, brushing kids elbows.

"Watch it, idiot!" someone said.

"Sorry," I replied and kept moving.

"Hey, freak! Is it time for yer poundin'?"

That statement, accompanied by a chorus of rude laughter, came from the back seats and was usually the beginning of a very long, painful and humiliating ride to school. I found a seat next to another victim and tried to make myself as small as I could while Willis seemed content to remain standing in the aisle. It wasn't too long after the bus started off again that the first shot was fired. It consisted of a spit wad that wedged behind my right ear. I removed the nasty thing and said nothing. This was followed by several ear ‘tweaks,’ rubber band assaults, and then, as usual, a ‘good morning’ head slap.

“Hey, freak, ya wanna take-a swing at me?”

That challenge came from Walter (Wally) Matson, a big dumb, brute of a farm kid who sadistically enjoyed tormenting me as well as a few others who rode the beast to school. He was supported by those who made up his ‘gang’ (several boys) who egged him on. Willis seemed fascinated by the exchange, until …

“Daniel, I am concerned. I sense that you are currently in an unhealthy state of distress,” he said, speaking out loud.

I quickly looked around to see if anyone heard him. And, to my surprise, nobody did.

“Hey, retard, how about a nice fat lip?” Wally threatened from a few seats behind me.

“Not today, thanks,” I replied over a shoulder.

“Daniel, I also detect that your heart rate is unusually high for a person of your age and I sense emotional conflict along with an increase in the secretions of your sweat glands, mainly in your arm pits, the back of your neck and …”

“Shut up, will ya?” I blurted out. Suddenly, the whole bus got quiet.

“How’s that, turd?” Wally barked. “Did you say somethin’?”

“Uh, no … sorry, my mistake,” I quickly replied.

"Mistake, huh? I'll say it was," Wally said as he got up and came forward. He stopped right next to me, turned to the kid behind him and ordered him to move over. The kid did, and Wally sat down across the narrow aisle from me.

"Maybe that fat lip I promised you might turn into something worse?" he said, tweaking my ear.

"Oh, Wally, leave 'em alone, will ya? He's not bothering you," one of the girls said.

"Shut up, skank!" he fired back at her. The girl huffed and turned around. "Now, where was I? Oh yeah, I was about to give the freak here a lesson in manners," he said, leaning in close to me.

"Daniel, I believe this fellow human means you harm physically and I would urge you to take evasive measures to assure your safety," Willis said.

"Oh, for cryin' out loud, what'da ya want me to do, zap 'em with my ray gun?" I blurted out yet again.

"Huh? Who you talkin' to, idiot?" Wally said angrily, giving me a shove.

"Nobody, look, just let me be, will ya?"

"No. I'm gonna smarten you up right now and then we'll talk some more in gym class," Wally threatened.

"That's an excellent idea, Daniel," Willis said, "zap him!"

I just shook my head at Willis.

“Are ya ready for that fat lip freak?” Wally said, balling up a fist.

“Daniel, use your little finger,” Willis said, holding up one of his.

“What?” I said.

“I said are ya ready for your fat lip?” Wally repeated. “Are you deaf, besides stupid?”

“Daniel, just take a deep breath and touch him,” Willis said calmly.

I looked into Wally’s eyes and my heart turned to ice. I wanted to cry even before I was hurt (I usually did) but, Willis just nodded at me. I stuck out my little finger and pointed it at Wally.

“Ya want me to break that first, do ya?” Wally laughed.

Then I touched him.

It felt like when you get out of a car sometimes, or walk across a carpet in stocking feet... that snap of electricity? I felt it go through my hand, but it didn’t hurt ... well, it didn’t hurt *me* anyway. Wally was another story. He was propelled, straight backward and across the kids lap sitting behind him. He yelped as he banged his head against the window. The poor kid he was on top of slid out from under him and quickly got outta the way. I just sat there and looked at my little finger in amazement as I flexed it.

Wally cursed and came at me. I closed my eyes, held out my arm and touched him again. This time it was worse ... for him. This time he hit the side of the bus with greater force knocking the wind outta him, his hair stuck straight out and he was covered with goose flesh.

"What the ..!" he cried out.

The bus driver looked up into his mirror and asked what was wrong.

"This freak tried to kill me, that's what!" Wally shouted.

"If you can't behave yourself, come up here and sit on the floor next to me," the driver barked.

Wally looked at me and I smiled back, flexing my little finger at him.

"Care for another?" I said evilly.

"You're dead meat!" he seethed.

"Am I?" I replied. I slid over next to him bringing my finger close to his face.

"Care for another?" I repeated.

Wally stared fearfully at my digit and tried to make himself part of the bus wall.

"Hey, Wally, what's goin' on man?" one of the other bullies said.

"Nothin' ... just get this freak away from me," Wally pleaded, the arrogance now gone.

"That's right, Walter," I whispered, trying to hold my temper, "I *am* a freak. Touch me ever again, in fact, if *any* of your pals bother me, or anyone else on this bus, I'm gonna touch you real good, understand?"

I put my little finger into his face and it miraculously snapped a small blue arch of current between my finger tip and the end of his nose causing him to yell and bang his head, again, against the window.

"Alright, what's goin' on back there?" the bus driver hollered.

"Nothing, sir," I replied, returning to my seat.

Wally Matson just sat there, bug-eyed, breathing heavily and trying to figure out what just happened. I looked up at Willis. He nodded with approval and flexed one of his long fingers at me in a form of salute. The rest of the kids on the bus didn't know what to make of the whole affair either, but by the time we pulled into the school yard I had several compliments on a job well done (whatever I did) and a few slaps on the back. No handshakes though, just in case. Wally and his pals waited until I got off the bus and kept their distance from then on.

I felt as though a great weight had been lifted off my back as I walked into school and the word spread. I later found myself alone in a boy's restroom, or at least I thought I was ... Willis had followed me in like a puppy.

“So, what happened back there on the bus?” I asked him as I stood in front of the porcelain and did my business.

“You defended yourself admirably,” he said.

“How? How’d I do that?”

“You zapped him with your ray gun, isn’t that what you wanted?”

“Ray gun? What ‘ray gun?’ It was my finger. I’ve never did that before in my life. What’d you do to me anyway?”

“I merely redirected and enhanced your naturally occurring bio-chemo-electrical current in your body through your smallest digit. You did the rest,” Willis replied.

“Huh? Oh, never mind. Uh, say, can I do it again if I need to?”

“Without my assistance? No. Humans, I’m afraid, due to their underdeveloped brain mass and lack of sufficient mental discipline, could never, on their own, begin to accomplish what you did, even at a rudimentary level.”

“So, yer sayin’ we’re stupid?” I replied, zipping up.

“Not at all,” Willis quickly responded. “Your race, surprisingly, has had, historically and technologically speaking, some rather outstanding accomplishments to its credit and, no doubt, have the potential to accomplish substantially more in the future.”

"Well, that's nice for the human race," I said, washing my hands, "I just wanna get through high school in one piece …."

Then the bell rang.

"Look, I gotta get to class. Tag along if you want, just …"

"I shall not be a distraction, Daniel," Willis promised. And, he wasn't. He just stood in the corner with his arms crossed and listened.

Finally, the day was over and we were on the bus for the ride back home. To my surprise, the boys in the back (Wally especially) sat quietly whispering among themselves. I turned around several times and they stopped. I looked over at Willis. He nodded, turned and walked to the rear of the bus, paused a moment, then came back. When we arrived at my house we got off the bus, I grabbed the newspaper outta the mailbox and Willis and I headed up the driveway.

"Why'd you go to the back of the bus?" I asked.

"Your friends were plotting foul play against you. I fixed it."

"Huh? You fixed it? How?"

"Well, simply put, I placed a thought into their impressionable minds. You shouldn't be bothered by them again," Willis said.

"Oh, yeah?" I smiled with relief, "For how long?"

"Why, for the rest of your life, Daniel."

I stopped and turned to him. "Are you sayin' those guys aren't gonna hassle me for the rest of my life?"

"That is correct," Willis replied.

I swore slightly and rubbed my forehead.

"You need nutrition, Daniel. Come, let us continue on to your dwelling and imbibe some cookies," Willis suggested, taking my arm. We continued walking. "It disturbs you, what I did? You disapprove?" he said as we walked.

"I ... dunno," I replied, not really knowing how to react. "It's just that they've ... I mean ..."

"Those boys have been a negative part of your life for so long that you are now concerned that you will not know how to feel from this point forward," Willis interjected.

"Yea, somethin' like that, I guess," I replied weakly.

"You will miss their abuse of you?"

"No! No, this is a dream come true, but ..."

"But?"

"I just never expected it to be cured like this, I guess."

"How would you have wanted it to be cured?"

"Well, I always imagined a fair fight. I would win and they would leave me alone."

“And you believe that?”

“Well, yeah. It’s like on T.V. The ‘good guy’ always wins and the ‘bad guy’ loses and goes away.”

Willis made his laughing noise. We stopped at the front porch.

“You are referring, of course, to your primitive electronic broadcasting form of mind control that is crudely designed to manipulate and misinterpret reality?”

“Uh, we just call it television,” I responded.

“Daniel, listen to me, there are no ‘good guys’ or ‘bad guys,’ just intelligent entities who randomly decide to make either logical or illogical decisions based on their perception of reality at any given time.”

“Huh? Look, Willis, ya really gotta dumb-it-down for me, okay? What’da ya talkin’ about?” I sighed.

“Daniel, your human history testifies to the fact that fighting amongst your species has accomplished, virtually, nothing. Otherwise, you would have outlawed war and aggression centuries ago. The problem is that your people have not yet acquired the intellect to see that conflict of any kind is counterproductive .... No one wins in the end. Human beings, based on what I have seen, lack a basic trait that would enable them to live in harmony with each other.”

“What’s that?”

“Respect … for one’s self and for others. Once that has become part of your species genetic code there will cease to be the ‘Wallys’ of your world … or the ‘Daniels’, for that matter.”

“What’da ya mean, ‘the Daniels?’”

“You, my immature friend, lack respect for yourself. Once you acquire that, then you will no longer need your ‘ray-gun.’”

“Well, how do I get that?”

“With time.”

“How much time?”

Willis smiled. “Time for cookies,” he replied.

We went inside, said, “Hi Mom” (or at least I did), raided the cookie jar and a glass of milk and went up to my room. I split the milk with Willis, who was not convinced that the white liquid actually came from an animal called a cow. And we talked. He told me some neat stuff about where he came from and his life there: how they haven’t had wars for millions of years … about how they enjoy traveling to other ‘realms’ (whatever he meant by that … I didn’t ask).

Later, I got called down to supper and chores. When I got back Willis was standing on my bed, bouncing slightly on the mattress.

“Welcome back, Daniel, this is stimulating,” he said as he bounced.

"Glad to hear it," I replied as I closed the door.

"Daniel, I have something to tell you," he said, stepping off the bed.

"So tell me already."

"I have to leave," he said flatly.

"Leave? Where?"

"I have to leave here very soon, I regret to say," he replied sadly.

"Your friends have found you?"

"Yes they have. I want to tell you that it has been a pleasure meeting you and riding your bus to school."

"Well, hang on, when're ya comin' back? You can come back to visit, right?"

Willis shook his head. "No."

I suddenly felt the urge to bawl as I rubbed my shirt sleeve across my nose.

"Daniel, I sense deep regret emanating from you. I'm sorry this information is distressing. I am also affected."

"Well, doggone it, Willis, I was just startin' to like you and now ..."

"How interesting," Willis replied. "When we first met, I sensed fear, uncertainty and hostility. Now it is different. Now, I sense ... respect. This is an accomplishment."

“Yeah, I get it,” I said.

Then I heard a noise. It seemed to fill the room and I looked around, wondering what was goin’ on.

“It is alright, Daniel. It is only my bus arriving to take me away,” Willis said, extending his hand to me.

I took it and we shook. He nodded and smiled. “Remember what we have discussed,” he said, backing away and stepping up onto the bed again.

“I will,” I said as the noise turned into a hum, and then Willis started to glow.

“Goodbye, Daniel, be well,” he said … and then he was gone.

“Bye, Willis, goodbye … I …”

I just stood there in shock I guess, not really knowing what to do. After a few minutes I went over and sat on my bed. It was warm where Willis had been standing. I guess I cried for a little while … and then I decided I had better write down everything I could remember about him and what he had told me when we were together. Afterward, I did my homework. It was midnight by the time I finished. I opened my bedroom window and climbed out onto the porch roof. I sat there in the chilly air and looked up at the night sky wondering where he was. My eyes filled up with water. After a short time, I yawned, went back inside and hit the sack.

Well, days turned into years. I graduated, went to college, got married, had kids, they grew up and left … and I grew older.

Occasionally, during my life, I thought about Willis, and at some point in my rise to intellectual maturity, I logically concluded that he had been merely an imaginary character that my sub-conscious had created in order to get me through a very difficult period in my adolescence. Soon I was convinced of it and later it became a conviction. So I filed Willis away and forgot about him.

I'm sixty now and I enjoy spending quiet time in my room, on my laptop, doing research and exploring the many wonders mankind has discovered in outer space. One night I was browsing the latest Hubble Space Telescope images. I was fascinated by what marvels exist out there in the universe. It was late. I took off my reading glasses and rubbed my eyes, yawned and decided to find my wife and go to bed. I stood up and walked to the door ... and that's when I heard a voice from behind me say:

"Hello, Daniel."

The Dhed Next Door

If you wanna talk about weird neighbors, we got 'em right next door. Yep, Mr. and Mrs. Dhed and their even weirder kid, Leroy. They moved in about a month ago and from then on, for some reason, things started happenin' all over the neighborhood. Things like pets missin' all of a sudden.

Mrs. Albertson, who lives down the street, put food out on her front porch one mornin' for her cat, like she always has, and when she came back, Fluffy was gone and never returned. The same thing happened to old man Wheeler's dog, just up and left ... kinda like Mrs. Wheeler did a year or so before, but I don't think one had to do with the other. Then there's Mrs. Grossvent's prize poodle, Caesar, who won some kinda dog show award that she endlessly twaddles about, it disappeared from its 'throne' (the sofa) while Mrs. Grossvent was in the shower. It really hit the fan then. She had the sheriff, the fire department, the dog catcher, and even the mayor at her house tryin' to calm her down. They finally had to haul her away, kickin' and screamin', in an ambulance, hooked up to an oxygen tank. It was quite a circus.

Oh, by the way, my name is Polly Warner and I live at 1201 Oaklawn Drive in the little town of Davensport, N.H. The Dheds moved into the old Victorian house around the corner from me, number 1313 Raven Lane (how appropriately weird). The first time I saw them they reminded me of The Adams Family (the T.V. show or somethin' similar)... they were just spooky right from the giddy-up. Their backyard was just over our backyard privacy fence and I could see the goings-on from my bedroom window. In fact, I had a good view of Leroy's room, which was on the second floor, and I could see him from time to time standing there and staring over at our place ... at me. I'd whip my curtains shut and rub the goose flesh off my arms. I'd complain to my parents but dad would just tell me to mind my own business and the Dheds would do the same. I dunno, I wasn't convinced about that. A little while later I heard barking. "Never heard that before," I said, poking my head out between my bedroom window curtains. Sure enough, the Dheds next door had a dog and it was a big one. I couldn't see it from behind our fence, but it was there barking at it.

"Oh great," I sighed. "Now I gotta spend the rest of my summer vacation listening to that thing."

Well, summer passed. There was about a week left before the inevitable return to school and I was hoping to spend it doing what I enjoy most, which is writing. You see, I'm a mystery writer ... well, an amateur one anyway. Although, I did win first prize from the local book club for Best New Author (they had a contest and I got a pie and a ribbon). My dad's a published author, and he's also the English teacher at our school. My mom works at the library in town as the head librarian. So I guess I come by 'word-smithing' naturally. I guess that's a perk. My dad says, "flipping your lip properly is ten-tenths of being successful in this life because nobody enjoys listening to an idiot." Mom would always roll her eyes when he would say that and then ask if we wanted seconds at supper. Actually, I just prefer being myself. My diction may not always be according to the book, but hey, I'm only fifteen, so gimme a break. Speaking of which, the summer break, as usual, was too short, and now I had to deal with academia for a whole 'nother year, well, at least 'till x-mas break.

I sat at my desk in front of my electric typewriter and banged away, that is, until that beast next door started in. Thoughts of horrifying dog deaths coursed through my brain.

"That does it," I said, standing up. I went to the window, opened it and stuck my head out. "Hey! Stuff a sock in it, will ya!" I hollered.

The barking stopped and I stood up. "Well, I guess I showed him," I said. Then I thought I heard someone yell back. I stuck my head back out the window.

" ... did ya hear me?" a voice finished.

"Who's that? Who's there?" I yelled back.

Then I saw this kid backing up holding on to the dog's collar as he did so.

"It's me, Leroy Dhed .... Hey, sorry about the noise. I'll try to shut 'em up," he said, attempting to wrestle with the brute. "What's yer name?"

"Polly," I replied, surprising myself that I gave him my name. Leroy Dhed was dressed in black, *all* black. Black jeans, black tee shirt, black shoes, and the shirt had large white skulls decorating the front of it.

"Nice shirt," I blurted facetiously. (It was really ugly.)

"Hey thanks, it's my favorite," he proudly replied.

Then I noticed something. "What's that around your neck?" I squinted.

"Oh, it's a choke collar."

"Are those ... spikes sticking outta it?" I said maneuvering my head to see it more clearly.

"Oh, yeah, I guess they are. You like it?"

"No. Aren't they for dogs?"

"Well, yeah, I suppose, but where I came from, this is cool."

"Well kid, it ain't gonna be cool here in Davensport, so I suggest you either lose the collar or wear a bag over your head .... The teachers will make you take it off, I'm tellin' ya," I warned.

"Oh ... well, I dunno ..." he replied as he fondled the thing. Then he lost his grip on the dog and it bolted away towards the house. "Look, I gotta go," Leroy said quickly. "Nice to meet you, Polly ... see ya around, maybe ..." he hollered as he charged after the delinquent dog.

"Maybe my foot, weirdo," I said to myself as I stood back up, shut the window tight, and pulled the curtains over it. "That kid's wearin' a dog collar?" I remarked, chuckling to myself. I went back to my desk and finished the evening off writing until bedtime.

The next few days were a blur. I got occupied with some last minute school shopping trips with mom and other things. During this time more weirdness was happening around town. Things like street lights exploding for no good reason, the power going out randomly for hours at a time (again for no good reason) and the strange disappearance of Homer 'Stinky' Cobb.

Homer Cobb was a fixture in Davensport since, well, before I was born. In fact, my dad remembered him from when he was a kid. The guy musta been ancient. He was the resident derelict (hobo) in the community. The story goes that he just decided to 'drop out' one day. He spent most of his time in the park, bumming around picking up bottles and cans. I guess he lived someplace (I was told in a shack in the woods). I never bothered to find out. What I do know for a fact is that you couldn't spend much time downwind from him, thus the name, 'Stinky.' I guess no one had seen him for a few days, which wasn't unusual, but what tipped the local cops off that something was wrong was the pair of worn out old boots he always wore laying on the push-go-round in the Kiddy Park. Somebody recognized them and called it in. They searched the area, even went to his shack, but no Homer Cobb. Dad talked about it one night at supper.

"Deputy Sheriff Malone said they found food and drink on a plate in the shack and some money stuffed under an old mattress. If the man decided to leave, why would he leave his money *and* his shoes?"

"I'm sure I have no idea," Mom replied. "Polly, come help with the dishes."

"Well, I'm just saying it's peculiar," Dad said, getting up. "I just hope the poor fellow hasn't been the victim of foul play. Oh, by the way, I need to go over to the school for a brief meeting, I shouldn't be too long."

"Don't get sucked up by the mother ship," I replied as I cleared the table.

"Polly?" he replied.

"Well, I'm just sayin' maybe old Stinky got himself sucked up."

Dad frowned at me. "You've been reading science fiction again, haven't you?" He smirked.

“No, not really. It’s just that everybody knows that this area has always been a prime location for ‘sightings’.”

“Oh really? Are you referring to U.F.O.’s?”

“Well, yeah.”

“Sweetheart, even if there were extraterrestrial visitors from some other planet, why would they ‘suck up’ old Homer Cobb?”

“Maybe he was just handy?” I smiled.

“Polly, go help your mother .... Evelyn, I’ll be back later,” Dad said, ending the conversation, and shaking his head at me. Then he turned and walked to the front door.

“Fine, dear!” Mom called from the kitchen. “Polly, load the dishwasher please.”

“Well, why not Homer Cobb?” I mumbled to myself as I carried a handful of plates out of the dining room.

Later that evening, I was in the backyard when I heard ...

“Pssst!”

“Who’s that?” I said, looking everywhere.

“Polly, it’s me, Leroy,” replied a voice from behind a crack in the wood fence.

I went over and stood next to it. “What’da ya want?” I asked.

“Nothin’, I just heard ya walkin’ around .... What’s up?”

“Nothing, just covering lawn furniture. What’re you doing?”

“Nothin’... well, just thinkin’,” he replied.

“About what?”

“School, and about what you told me.”

“Oh, you mean about you not wearing a dog collar to school? That’s good advice,” I said.

“Well, that’s just it ... I kinda gotta wear it.”

“Huh? What’da ya mean you gotta wear it?”

I heard him walking around and it sounded like he was kicking at the ground.

“Where’s your dog?” I asked.

“Oh, he’s inside.”

“Sooo, what’s his name?”

“Uhh ... it’s Gronk.”

“Gronk? What kinda name is that for a dog?” I giggled.

“Yeah,” Leroy laughed, “kinda dumb, I know ... it means ‘eater,’ I think.”

“Wait, Gronk means ‘eater’? In what language?”

I didn’t hear anything for a while.

"Leroy, you still there?"

"Yeah."

"So, what's goin' on with you? You sound freaked, everything alright?" I asked, stepping up to the fence and putting my right eye up to the crack. I could see Leroy pacing back and forth on the lawn. He was still dressed in black to match his mop of black hair … and fingernails? (You've gotta be kiddin'?)

"No … I dunno, just nervous I guess," he replied, shoving both hands deep into his pockets.

"Look, it's just the first day of school jitters and you're new here. Just relax, will ya? Uh, lemme ask, don't you have any other cloths to wear?"

Leroy stopped pacing and looked at the fence. "You can see me?" he said, coming over.

"Yeah, I can see ya. You really gotta lose those black clothes, and for cryin' out loud, black fingernails?"

He looked quickly at his hands and then shoved them back into his pockets.

"I'll bet you think I'm weird, huh?"

"Weirdest dude I've ever seen in these parts. Where you from anyway?"

Leroy hesitated. "California."

"Bull," I replied.

"Well, Boston then. Look, does it matter?" he said,

looking straight at me through the crack with one eye. And, what an eye it was ... the brightest green I've ever seen. I whistled without thinking.

"What?" he responded.

"Where'd you get those peepers?" I asked.

"Huh?"

"Your eyes. They're, well, great," I said.

"Oh, thanks," he replied, stepping back a few feet, "and, no, I don't have any other clothes.

"Well, you can go to the mall and buy some, ya know?"

He looked around behind him as if he was being watched. "Nah, I'll be okay, I guess ... say look, Polly, could you, I mean, would you mind kinda showin' me the ropes tomorrow? At school I mean?"

Now I stepped backward.

"Uhh, well, I ..."

"Look, I understand if I creep you out, but, I'm kinda lost here and, well ... okay, look, never mind, it was just-a thought.

"Wait!" I replied, stepping back up to the fence, "I didn't say no did I?"

"Well, you didn't say yes."

"Okay, I'll get you through the first day, but after that you're on your own, got it?"

"Yeah, yes, thanks!" he smiled. He had a nice smile too, nice straight teeth. "So, is there a bus or..?"

"Nope, it's supposed to be a nice day tomorrow. We walk. Meet me out in front of my house at 7:00 sharp. Don't be late or I'll leave without you."

"Okay, sure, 7:00 it is," he replied. He waved, briefly, and then turned and walked back to his house. I stood there and watched him go, then I went inside, kicking myself for agreeing to buddy up with this Dhed guy. I couldn't wait for the fallout from this.

The first day of school came early and so did Leroy. I looked out my front window and there he was, black from head to toe, again. Even his cap and backpack where black and I could see he was wearing that dog collar. I sighed audibly and looked heavenward for help.

"Polly? Are you alright?" my mother asked. "Do you want a ride to school? I can drive you."

I thought about it, I really did.

"Nah, I'll walk, prolly pick up a few friends along the way. See ya this afternoon," I replied as cheerfully as I could.

"Very well, dear, have a good first day."

I walked out the front door and closed it behind me. Then I made eye contact with Leroy. He pushed the hair away from his face, smiled and waved.

"Morning, Polly," he said.

I adjusted my backpack, set my jaw and walked up to him.

"Look, Leroy, let's get one thing straight," I began, "I'm just doing this as a favor ... a onetime favor, understand?"

"Sure, sure, Polly, I understand."

"And, another thing, when we get to school, we don't know each other ... and don't call me by my first name, ever, got it?"

"Yeah, I get it. Not in your clique, right?" he replied somberly, hanging his head and walking away.

"Hey, school's this way," I gestured with my thumb in the opposite direction.

Leroy huffed, turned back around and walked past me. I sighed, looked up at the sky, shook my head and followed. He was taller than me and had a longer stride. I began to have trouble keeping up.

"Leroy, slow up!" I said.

"Don't call me by my first name either," he angrily said over his shoulder.

I felt like an idiot. "Okay, look, you gotta cut me some slack. I live here and ..."

"Yeah, I know all about it. This ain't my first school. I'm the 'Dhed next door' ... ha ha, I've heard it all before. Just point me to the school."

“It’s down two more blocks, turn right, you’ll see the ball field, main building’s the big one on the left,” I replied. I felt my face get red and my stomach hurt. “Hey, I’m … I’m sorry, okay? Hold up, will ya?”

Leroy stopped, slung his pack over the opposite shoulder and waited. “Look, I don’t wanna be anyone’s charity case,” he replied with disgust.

I stood next to him and rubbed my nose. “You’re not. You’re my neighbor,” I replied. “Let’s go,” I said, with a crooked smile.

He didn’t seem sure at first, then he smiled back and we walked together.

“So, where’re you from really?” I asked.

He looked over at me but didn’t reply.

“What’s the big secret, guy?” I pressed. “Why can’t you tell me?”

“My parents told me not to say … it’s private,” he answered.

“I’m sorry, but that’s weird.”

“Maybe so, but … you wouldn’t believe me if I told you, so don’t ask, okay?”

“Oh really? Try me,” I challenged.

“Why? Why should I trust you?” he said.

“Hey, I’m putting my rep on the line for you today and *you* don’t trust me?”

“Oh, is that what this is about, your rep?”

“Yeah, it is. Now stop playin’ dumb and just spit it out.”

Leroy stopped abruptly and looked around. There were some other kids walking across the street, he seemed to wait until they passed by.

“Look, you gotta promise me that you won’t tell anyone,” he said, his green eyes burning a hole through my face.

“Okay, don’t rupture a nerve. I promise,” I replied.

“Let’s keep walking,” he said, looking behind him.

“You’re creepin’ me out.”

“Sorry. Okay, here goes,” he said, then he cleared his throat several times. “I’m not from here ...”

“Well, no kidding. I watched you guys move in and ...”

“Polly, just listen, will ya?”

“Sorry. You were saying?”

“I, I mean *we*, that is my parents and I, are from ... someplace else.”

“Yeah, you said Boston.”

“I lied.”

“Figured that too.”

“We’re not from this ...” he stopped and rubbed his face.

“This country right?” I interrupted. “So, you’re foreigners. Where you from, Europe? That’s cool,” I said, trying to be positive.

“No, not Europe.”

“Where? Africa, Asia?”

“Sagittarius,” he said flatly.

I looked up at him. “I don’t remember a country called that off hand. Was it part of the former Soviet Union or ...”

“No Polly, it’s a dwarf elliptical galaxy 80,000 light years from this solar system,” he said looking straight ahead.

We walked a few more steps and then I socked him a good one in the shoulder.

“*Ouch!* Hey!” he yelped.

“Look, idiot,” I blurted angrily, “I’m trying to be nice to you and you tell me you’re from ... from outer space?”

“I said you wouldn’t believe me. See? I was right.”

“Are you serious? Of course I don’t believe you. I dunno why I bothered to help you ... you walk the rest of the way by yourself,” I huffed. Then I saw a couple of girls I knew walking down the opposite street and waved at them.

“Hi, Polly!” they yelled back.

I gave Leroy an evil look and left him standing there while I ran across the road to join my friends. Leroy walked on alone and I didn’t see him the rest of the day or the next few days, but I sure heard about him ....

“You’ve got yourself a real creep-o-zoid for a neighbor, Polly,” my girlfriend Valerie said over the phone.

“Oh yeah, how do ya figure?” I replied as I sat at my desk in my room looking over a chapter in American History.

“Are you kiddin’? Didn’t you hear what happened in Mr. Beeker’s science class the other day?”

“It’s Bercher, and no I didn’t, enlighten me.”

“Well, I heard from someone whose boyfriend was in the class with ‘Dead Meat’ ... by the way, that’s what everyone’s callin’ him. Anyway, they said that somehow he caused all the chemicals to start boilin’ and spillin’ all over the place, everybody had to leave the room until the smoke cleared. There was that. And then I heard from Mandy Pular that Denise Bradford’s boyfriend said that Dead Meat wouldn’t change his cloths for gym or take off that awful dog collar he wears. Coach Bosco sent him to the principal’s office and ...”

Valerie went on endlessly it seemed like, until ...

"Uh, look, Val, this is all interesting, but the kid's name is Leroy and yeah, he's a little weird, but he's from, well, Boston, and he's just used to being *there* and now he's *here* in Nowheresville. I think we just need to cut him some slack and ..."

"Ohhh, sounds to me like somebody likes Leeeroy!"

"Knock it off will ya? I don't need the drama. I just don't think it's fair that the new kid needs to be harassed the first week of school, that's all."

"Fine, fine, okay, I was just lettin' you know what was goin' on seein' as how Leeeroy Dead is your next door neighbor ... hey, that's cute: the dead next door!"

I held the phone away from my ear while Valarie guffawed like a dope ... she can be sooo annoying sometimes.

"Oh, God," she interrupted herself, "my braces are killin' me, I gotta go brush my teeth," she said, making clicking noises with her mouth.

"Fine, Val, and by the way, his name is spelled D.h.e.d., I read it on their mailbox," I said.

"It's still pronounced 'Dead', so what?"

"Nothing ... look, I gotta read these chapters. Call me later or I'll see ya on Monday, okay?"

"Okay, Polly, be good. Ciao!"

I hung up the phone, sighed deeply and tried to get back into the reading, but the words just seemed to run together. I sat there with my chin cradled in my hand. Then I startled myself when my eyes ran across a word that looked like ... "Sagittarius?" I said out loud. Then I blinked my eyes and looked closer. "Saginaw ..." I repeated several times. "It's Saginaw, you dope," I said to myself. After that I was in no mood to read any longer. What I did do was go downstairs and ask my father for some of his books on astronomy.

"What're you looking for, sweetheart?" he asked as he sat there behind his desk in his office grading papers.

"Sagittarius," I replied.

He stood up, perused the wall of books behind him, pulled down several volumes and handed them to me. "Look at the glossaries in the back, I'm sure you'll find it there," he said. I stared down at the cover of one of the books that featured a color picture of the Milky Way.

"Something else, Polly?" he asked.

"Dad, do you think it's possible that there could be, well, life in other galaxies?" I asked.

"What brought this up? Something in school?" he asked.

"Yeah, some kids were talking. What do you think?"

He paused and rubbed the back of his neck. "Sweetheart, centuries ago everyone knew the earth was the center of the universe and everything, including the Sun, revolved around us ... and people were content with that knowledge. Then Galileo invented the telescope and blew that long held belief right out of the water. Now, here we are in the 1980s and everything is changing again. I understand that someday we're all going to have personal computers to run our lives with and who knows what else ... it's science fiction come to life. Some people will welcome it and some, like in Galileo's day, will not. As far as life beyond our solar system, well, who knows? Do I think it's possible? Yes, why not? Do others? No. We'll just have to wait and see what the future Galileos discover and then we had all better be ready to accept it."

"Dad, do you think it's possible that people from other worlds would visit us ... I mean someday?" I asked.

"Well, from what I understand, the scientists involved in the SETI program believe it. Some of our tax dollars are being used for this research ... messages being sent into space ... well, if anyone out there is listening maybe they'll give us a call someday. Again, who knows."

"Do you think if that ever happens, I mean if they visit, that they'll be ... dangerous?"

"Have you been watching horror movies?" he asked with a smile.

"No! Oh, no, but I was just wondering, that's all."

"Polly, use your logic. Any race advanced enough to make the trip millions of light years to our little world would certainly do so, in my opinion, with good intentions … but I could be wrong."

"What'da ya mean?"

"I mean they could come all that way to eat our brains! *Arrrr!"* he roared and grabbed me in a bear hug. I screamed and giggled and we both had a good laugh.

"I love you, Polly," he said, kissing me on my forehead, "you just keep being curious and asking questions. Now, I need to grade these papers before Monday, return the books when you're finished."

"I will, Dad … and thanks."

"You're welcome, sweetheart. Oh, by the way, are you starting to write another book?"

"Maybe," I replied. "Maybe this is research."

"Well good. If you need any help, ask."

"I will, Dad, thanks."

I left my father's room, went back upstairs and poured over everything I could find on the galaxy of Sagittarius. And there wasn't a whole lot, just size, distance and a few photos. I looked up out of my window and saw Leroy's bedroom light on. I walked over, stood in front of my window, and looked across. I just stood there for a long time; I don't know why either. Finally, he came and looked out. He just stood there too; we both did, just staring across the void of our backyards at each other. I could see his eyes, even from this distance, large and green and so clear that I got lost in them … then I could feel his breath on my cheek, his hands on my shoulders as he looked at me and smiled with those straight, perfect teeth I would kill to have in my mouth. "Polly." I heard him whisper to me, his voice echoing in my head as we floated in the vacuum of space, holding on to each other and tumbling over and over and ...

I sat straight up in bed, breathing heavily. The room was pitch dark and I still had my clothes on. I held my head for a moment, then swung my legs over the edge and stood up. I felt like when I had that half-a bottle of beer at the class picnic last year (my parents never found out). I walked over to the window and looked out. Leroy's room was dark. I waited for a few moments, felt stupid and turned to go to the bathroom, and then suddenly, I heard something hit my window. I stopped and listened. After a few moments, I heard it again. I went over and opened the window. The September night air was cool as I looked down, trying to see what was causing the noise.

"*Pssst, Polly!*" I heard a voice in the darkness below call.

"Leroy?" I whispered as loud as I could. "Is that you?"

"Yeah."

"What'da ya doing? You know what time it is?"

"Yeah, I do."

"What'da ya want?"

"I wanted to say goodbye."

"Goodbye? Where you goin'?"

"Away ... far away from here."

"What?! You're running away from home? Are you nuts?"

"No, Polly, I'm running away from here *to* my home."

"Huh? You're not making sense .... Just wait, I'm comin' down!"

I opened my bedroom door as quietly as I could and tip-toed past my parents' room, down the stairs and out the back door to the yard. I left the light off. The stars filled the night sky. I practically bumped into Leroy who was standing a few feet away.

"How'd you get over the fence?" I whispered.

"Never mind that ... look, I have to leave soon, tonight," he said anxiously.

"Leroy, I know you're having problems at school, but running away is not going to solve anything."

"No, Polly, you don't understand. It has nothing to do with school."

"It's your parents then?"

"They're *not* my parents."

"They're not? Who are they, relatives?"

"No. They're my 'keepers,' my jailers ...." He sighed and looked up at the sky.

“Look,” I said, “I know how sometimes adults can be insensitive and real pains but ...”

“Polly, listen to me. I tried to tell you on our way to school. I’m not from here, from this world. I don’t even belong in this form, this body. I’m trapped here.”

“Leroy, are you doing drugs?”

“No!” he replied, exasperated. He turned and walked a few steps away, shoving his hands into his pockets.

“Oh swell,” I said to myself, “my neighbor’s a junkie ...”

I walked over to him and discovered he was crying.

“Leroy ... hey, take it easy, will ya? I’m right here. We can work this out, okay?”

“I need your help, Polly. I can’t do this alone,” he sobbed, looking over at me.

“Help you with what?”

“I need you to take off this collar.”

“So take it off. What’s the big deal?”

“No, you don’t understand, *I* can’t ... but *you* can.”

“Why? What’s so special about it, about me?”

He turned to me and looked down. I could see his green eyes in the dark and he was making me nervous.

“Polly, I’m sorry, but I did something bad and I want you to know that I’m sorry.”

"Leroy, you're wiggin' me out, man. What'd you do, knock over a liquor store?"

"No. No, Polly, I ... I probed you ...."

"What?!" I squawked out loud.

"*Shhhh*, be quiet, or you'll wake Gronk!" Leroy whispered urgently.

"You mean the dog? He can't get over the fence!" I snapped back as quietly as I could.

"Yes, he can anytime he wants too. He can melt right through it to get to me ... or you."

"Leroy, you're scaring me," I said, trying to keep it together. "What'd you mean when you said you 'probed me'?

He looked up to the sky again and sighed. "You had a dream tonight, didn't you? A dream about us, embracing and floating in space, right?"

I shoved him away. "How'd you know that, huh? How would you know that?" I stammered.

"Because *I* gave you that dream, Polly. I had to see if you were compatible. I had to see if you were capable of helping me, of freeing me. And you are! You are, Polly. Yes, you're young, but you can do it. Will you help me to be free?"

"Free? I don't understand what you mean?"

"Then listen to me please and believe me."

"Okay, I'm listening."

"I told you that I'm from Sagittarius, another galaxy."

"I know where it is."

"That's good," he replied, his voice seemed deeper now and older. "My race is not like yours, physically speaking, but we share the same virtues and emotions. There was a conflict on my world, the reasons don't matter, but I was captured, abducted, and held against my will. My people kept trying to find me and they almost succeeded, but my captors took me far away, outside our own galaxy and found this place, Earth .... Who would have imagined this planet even existed? Anyway, we adapted to your species but we have to move around from place to place. You see, we have a problem with this form, this body. We generate a naturally occurring effect that we can't control in this environment. It causes, well, strange things to happen."

"You mean like in the science lab at school?"

"Yes, like that."

"I heard you wouldn't change into gym clothes."

"I can't."

"How come?"

Leroy thought for a moment, then unzipped his jacket and lifted up his tee shirt. I put my hand over my mouth and held my breath. His chest ... Leroy's bare chest was glowing the most beautiful green glow!

"Oh my God!" I whispered when I finally could breathe again. "Leroy, oh my God ... what? I mean ..."

"Do you believe me now, Polly?" he asked quietly.

I started to cry and couldn't stop. I just stood there and vibrated.

"I'm sorry, Polly. I'm so sorry, but I need your help," he pleaded.

I took several deep breaths and sucked it up. "Okay, keep talkin'," I stammered.

"Needless to say, we don't stay in any one place for long; people get suspicious and ask questions."

"Leroy, what happened to some of the pets ... and Homer Cobb?"

Leroy hung his head. "Gronk needs food from time to time ...."

I turned away and sobbed some more. After a few minutes I felt Leroy's hand on my back.

"Polly, listen to me. I have a window of opportunity tonight and I need your help."

I turned to him, wiping my face dry with my hands. "What can I do?"

"I need you to assist me in taking off this restraint ... this collar."

"Why, what does it do?"

"It keeps me bound to *them*," he said, looking over at his house. "It keeps me in this form so that I can't get away, but you can remove it for me. It will be difficult. There will be some ... pain involved, but I know you can succeed."

"Won't they chase you?"

Leroy took my shoulders. "Not if you stop them for me."

"How?"

"I'll show you, but ..."

"But what? Tell me."

"It will mean causing their deaths."

I caught my breath and stood back, looking up at him.

"You want me to *kill* them?"

"No, Polly, not directly, but you will cause them to be destroyed and I will be free."

I turned my back to him again. My head swam with indecision.

"Leroy, I'm ... I'm just a girl, a high school girl ... a kid ...."

"Yes ... and more," he said from behind me. "You are capable of more, but it's your decision, I can't force you."

We both stood there for a long time and said

nothing. Finally I turned around.

"Leroy, have they ... have they killed other people, other humans?"

"Regrettably, yes. Others, like your Mr. Cobb, have disappeared."

I rubbed my forehead. "Then I'll help you. I'll do it, Leroy."

Leroy smiled and took my shoulders again. "Thank you, Polly. Now we must hurry, come," he said, taking my hand.

"Where're we going?" I asked.

"The ball field at the school, it has a clear view of the night sky," he replied as we ran out of the yard and down the sidewalk towards the school. We were about halfway there when the street lights went out. Leroy stopped and seemed to be listening.

"They've missed me, they know I'm gone, we have to hurry. Hurry, Polly!" he said urgently, and we both ran for all we were worth. My lungs were burning by the time we got to the ball field. We tried to find the gate but it was dark.

"It's down farther," I said as we felt along the chain link. "Why can't we just do it here?" I asked.

"Too much interference, I need an open area ... so many meters in diameter. Come, hurry!" he urged.

That's when we heard the dog howl in the darkness behind us.

"Gronk," Leroy said in despair. "We can't let him get to us."

"Yeah, I don't wanna get dog bit," I said.

"No, he'll kill you ..."

"Huh?"

"I found it!" Leroy said, flipping the latch and opening the gate. He shoved it closed behind us and we ran to the pitcher's mound.

The bales of the beast were getting louder as we stood there drenched in sweat facing each other. Leroy then took something out of his pocket wrapped in a cloth. It was two, jewel-like orbs, about the size of golf balls, one red and one green. He handed me the red one.

"Put this in your pocket for now," he said. I did, and then he looked up into the sky, clutching the green orb in one hand. "It's almost time, the barrier between galaxies will be the thinnest shortly, then I must go. Now, listen to me carefully, Polly. I need you to remove this collar. Use both hands, there's a clasp in back that pulls it apart. Once you start, though, don't stop until you have completely taken it off of me. When you do, throw it as far away from us as you can. Do you understand so far?"

"What happens if I stop? What happens if that dog gets here and ..?"

"We die, Polly," he replied, urgently, "You, me, the school; the neighborhood for a mile in diameter will evaporate. Do you understand?"

“Leroy, my God, what’re you saying, I ...”

“Polly, you can do this, I know you can. I trust you. Now, once the collar is off and I’m gone, take the red ball I gave you and throw it at Gronk, you don’t have to hit him, just throw it at him or any others that are with him. It will stop them from following me.”

“You mean they’ll die?”

“Yes.”

The dog was getting closer. Leroy now began to shed his clothing. “I drugged them all as best I knew how,” he said as he undressed, “but it won’t slow them up now that they know what I’m doing. We have to hurry.”

He took off every last stitch of clothing and stood there, naked, except for his collar. He clutched the green orb to his chest and they both seemed to pulsate together, like a heartbeat.

“Now, Polly, remove the collar; hurry!”

I stepped up close to him, feeling his body against mine. I reached around behind his neck and found the clasp.

“Hurry, Polly!” he urged into my ear.

I started to pull the clasp apart and that’s when the pain struck. It felt like a bolt of electricity shooting through my arms. I screamed in pain as wave after wave of current coursed down my arms and into my body.

"Don't let go, Polly! You can do this!" Leroy pleaded, over and over into my ear as I worked the collar apart.

I felt as if my arms were on fire and my heart was about to explode right through my chest.

"Hurry, Polly .... Gronk!" I heard Leroy shout. Then I yanked the collar off his neck and threw it as far as I could. Leroy screamed both in agony and relief it seemed as his entire body shuddered and glowed bright green, then orange, as his flesh peeled away from him in smoldering strips. I screamed at the spectacle, backing up from the pitcher's mound. An instant later, Leroy Dhed was gone in a flame of what looked like heaven's fire, piercing upward into the sky with a loud crack that resounded like thunder. Then I remembered ... Gronk!

I turned just in time to see glowing eyes bearing down on me. I screamed and reached into my pocket for the red orb. I also thought I saw two other people behind the dog, but I couldn't be sure because Gronk now was only a few feet away. I pulled out the orb and threw it at the dog. I heard someone yell, *"No!"* and then there was dazzling light and more screaming. I wasn't sure if it was me, the others, or the dog ... all I know is, when I woke up, I was in the I.C.U. of the local hospital with my parents looking down. I could hear voices talking around me, but I couldn't make out words clearly, at least not right away, but then ...

"It's going to take a few weeks for the burns to heal. They're not as severe as we originally thought, especially after a lightning strike like your daughter has experienced. I can tell you that her heart is good and her x-rays and brain scans appear normal, but we'll keep an eye on her periodically just to make sure," a man's voice said.

I heard my father say, "Thank you, Doctor, we really appreciate all your hard work."

I heard a woman agree ... it was my mom, and she was crying.

A few days later I was in a private room and able to receive visitors. Some of my friends from school brought me a huge card that everyone signed ... even some of the kids who I thought didn't like me scrawled 'get well.' Then later came explanation time, and why I was out there on the school ball field at 3:00 in the morning. I just said I was fascinated with the night sky and was told that was the best place to view it. That seemed to satisfy most folks but my dad is still skeptical to this day.

They still can't figure out what caused the city wide power outage, or the freak lightning strike that sun burnt my face, hands and ruined a perfectly good pair of sneakers ... or why the Dheds next door to us moved suddenly that night, never to be heard from again. And I guess they never will. I know *I* won't say anything. But I will say this: when I finally got to go home and sleep in my own bed again I remember getting up one night and standing at my bedroom window, looking over at the now empty house across from our back yard. I remember standing there and wondering about Leroy Dhed. Then, I was struck ... by what, I couldn't tell you, but all of a sudden I was suspended in the vastness of space with a bright galaxy lying outstretched before me. It was so magnificent I couldn't breathe. I felt someone behind me take my shoulders and turn me around. I saw bright green eyes and a mouth with perfect straight teeth that I would kill to have. The mouth smiled warmly at me and whispered. "Thank you, Polly!" It was Leroy's happy voice washing over me like waves. The mouth came closer and kissed me, my first kiss, and I felt warm all over. I smiled back and said, "You're welcome."

"Goodbye, Polly," the mouth said, and then he let me go and I fell backward and ... woke up!

I stood there alone in the darkness of my bedroom, my heart beating a hole through my chest. I cried, and then smiled through my tears. Leroy, I knew was free now... he was home and I helped him get there. I'll never forget that experience. Even years later, as I work as director at the Haden Planetarium, I sometimes have the opportunity to sit alone and gaze through the optics of the great telescope, looking at Sagittarius, wondering about Leroy ... the Dhed next door.

In-laws and Aliens

“Just remember, Antoni, when you marry, you don’t just marry the girl, you marry the whole family. *Capice*?”

“Yes, Uncle Mike,” I replied, trying not to laugh.

“You think I’m joking, eh? Well, I’m not. You listen good to me, boy. I was married forty-five years … to the same woman! And I tell you right now, and twice on Sunday, if I wasn’t a cop, I would’ve shot every single one of her relatives, starting with her mother, God help us, and made it look like an accident.”

“Uh, how’da ya shoot that many people, Uncle Mike, and make it look like an accident?” I asked, holding my face in one hand.

“You just never mind wise guy. I know things! This is Brooklyn. Things happen here … strange things. Why, when I was walkin’ a beat one time I …”

“Sorry, Uncle Mike, but I gotta run,” I interrupted and grabbed my coat hanging off a kitchen chair. “I promised Mom and Laurie I’d stop by the Deli and pick up some pepperoni and a few other things. They’re making pizza.”

“Pizza? Homemade?” the old guy smiled greedily; maybe I should go with you to help, eh?”

I held both hands up. “I was told to stop here, give you your prescription from the pharmacy, get the pepperoni and come back alone. We want to have a quiet dinner together, just Laurie, Mom, me and Laurie’s parents; they’re coming over from Long Island to meet Mom.”

“Oh, so now I’m too noisy or nosey, uh?”

“Probably both. Look, we’ll stop by later if we can, *capice*?”

“Yeah, yeah, *andare avanti*, get going. Kiss your mother for me, eh?”

“Sure, Uncle Mike, *arrivederci* ... see you later.”

“You kiss Laurie good for me to, eh?”

“Okay! *Ciao*!” I waved goodbye and quickly left the apartment, chuckling to myself. My Uncle Mike was a riot and I loved him dearly.

It was a pretty summer night in the city and people were out. There were couples walking arm in arm, some on the town dressed in fine clothes waiting for cabs or limos. Others out walking their dogs, or running, or ...

"Hey! Watch it!" I hollered at a couple of kids on rollerblades as they skated carelessly past me. "Idiots," I murmured to myself as I made the corner and headed down another busy street. The traffic was unusually light for a Friday night as I hurried across the street and down the sidewalk towards the delicatessen. I made it there in good time and walked in.

I loved the smell of the place ever since I was a kid growing up in the neighborhood. The aromas of fresh meats and spices filled the air in the brightly lit deli with its seemingly endless rows of white reach in coolers with curved glass, always shiny and always loaded with the best New York City had to offer. A little bell rang announcing my entry.

"Hey, Antoni! *Bello vederti*!" a large, red-faced man shouted in greeting from behind the counter. "What you need, eh? How's yoo momma?"

"*Malto bene,*" I replied, coming up to the counter. "Gino, I have a list." I handed the paper to him over the display.

"Ahhh, you gonna make a pizza-pie, eh? I get this for you as soon as I finish with Mrs. Rossi," he replied, nodding at an older woman standing down the aisle from me. The old lady smiled and tightened her *babushka* (the scarf she wore around her head).

"Hello, Mrs. Rossi," I smiled over at her.

"Hello, Antoni. Where's that beautiful girl of yours?"

"She's home with my mom. I'll tell her you said hi."

Mrs. Rossi smiled and nodded, then she began to wag a crooked finger at me. "You better marry that girl soon before she get old like me, *capice*?" She cackled.

"Mrs. Rossi, leave the boy alone, eh? He gonna get married soon enough," Gino said gregariously as he handed the old woman something wrapped in butcher paper. "There you go, Mrs. Rossi, *mangiare bene* ... eat good!"

"*Grazi, Gino*," she replied as she tucked the package under her arm and ambled toward me. She stopped briefly in front of me, reached up and pinched my cheek until tears formed in my eyes.

"You be good boy, eh?" she said.

"Yes, Mrs. Rossi," I answered respectfully. She nodded and left.

"I have your order coming right up, Antoni," Gino said as he worked behind the counter.

"Great!" I replied, nosing around the place.

"This a lot o-topping for two people, Antoni, who your momma cooking for, eh?"

"Oh, Laurie's parents are visiting us for the first time from Long Island," I said. "Mom's got the dough all ready to pop into the oven, soon as I get myself home."

“I bet you nervous, eh?”

“Yeah, kinda.”

“And now you ready to go, here!” Gino announced with a big smile as he plopped a paper wrapped package on top of a cooler. “You get going, I send the bill later, *capice*?”

I grabbed the package filled with meats. “Thanks, Gino. See you later, *addio*!”

“*Addio,* Antoni. Enjoy!” Gino waved goodbye as I left the deli and bolted for home several blocks away.

I walked in the door to our apartment and …

“Antoni, *mio dio,* where have you been? The dough is ready and the oven is hot,” my mother scolded.

“I got here as fast as I could, momma, okay? Where’s Laurie?”

“Here, give me that,” she said, taking the package from me. “She took her car and went to pick up her parents at the station, cabs are expensive. You makin’ me crazy! Now, go wash your hands and come help me in the kitchen.”

Sometime later, the smell of pizza filled the apartment, and a short time after that, the front door opened, spilling into the room a petite, dark haired young woman followed by two older adults.

“Ahh, they are here!” my mother squealed, whipping her hands on her already stained apron. “Antoni, where are you?” she yelled.

"I'll go find him, Maria," the young woman volunteered.

"Hello, Maria, it's a pleasure to finally meet you," the older man said warmly.

"Yes, so nice to meet you, Maria, our daughter speaks very highly of you. Thank you for inviting us over," the older woman added, coming over and hugging my mom.

"Yes, yes, it was the children's idea *and* a surprise to me ... so sudden! Young people these days. Now, let me remember, you are George and Gracie, yes?"

The older couple nodded.

"Wonderful! Well come in, come in. Make yourselves at home. We eat as soon as Laurie finds my son, he can't be too far in this small place!" my mother joked, and they all shared laughter.

In the meantime, I was in the bathroom shaving. I was making the final pass with my late father's straight razor when I heard a gentle knock at the door.

"Anyone home?" a familiar, female voice, inquired.

"Nobody here but us Italians," I replied, then I reached over and opened the door.

Laurie came in, looked at me, giggled mischievously, then threw her arms around my neck. She kissed me full on the mouth, resulting in decorating her face with shaving cream. We laughed as I took a damp towel and wiped both our faces off with it.

"Miss me?" she asked.

"You weren't gone that long for me to miss you, sweetheart," I replied. "And I'm starving."

"Me too, it smells so good back there ... your mom made pasta too," Laurie added.

"Hmm, let's go!" I said and hustled us both out.

The food was *perfetto*! My mother was a wonderful cook and was told so many times over the course of the evening, as we all sat around the table and filled ourselves with large slabs of pizza, spaghetti, garlic bread and a favorite family vino. A little later, while we were all digesting and sipping our wine, Laurie kept giving me the eye and little head nods. I thought I knew what she meant, but I wasn't sure until she kicked me under the table.

"Well, folks," I suddenly and painfully interrupted, "I, that is Laurie and I, have an announcement to make."

"An announcement?" my mother parroted, with a look of surprise, "what announcement, Antoni?"

"Well, uhhh ..." I hesitated too long.

"Mom, Dad, Maria," Laurie cut in, "Anthony and I wanted to take this opportunity to let you know that we are expecting ..."

“Oh my God! Antoni!” my mother yelped, standing up and putting a hand on her forehead, “tell me you haven’t brought disgrace on our family name? *Mio dio*, if your papa were here he would hit the roof and …”

“Ma! Take it easy, will ya? Laurie’s *not* pregnant. What gave you that idea?” I said with embarrassment.

“She said ‘expecting,’ I know what ‘expecting’ means,” Mom said, wagging her finger at Laurie.

“No, no, Maria,” Laurie interjected nervously, “You didn’t let me finish. Please, Maria, please sit down,” she urged.

Mom sat back down and took a good slug of wine, while Laurie’s parents just sat there smiling tightly and waiting.

“Anthony?” Laurie said looking at me and jabbing her head in a particular direction.

“Okay,” I began again, “we, that is Laurie and I, wanted you folks to know (I took a deep breath) that we’ve decided to get married this fall ….”

“Probably sometime in October,” Laurie quickly added.

“Married! Married?” my mother replied painfully, as if she’d been slapped. “Since when? You have only known each other a few weeks. And now you want to get married? Antoni, are you engaged? Is she Catholic? You don’t tell your mother nothing?”

Now I took a slug of wine. "Well, Ma, look, we *are* engaged, kinda ... in other words, I asked Laurie to marry me and she said yes and ..."

"So, where's the ring, Antoni?" my mother said, looking at Laurie's hand.

"I don't have one, Maria," Laurie said.

"But, she will, we've talked about it. I just haven't had the money ... but I will. I want us to pick a nice set out together and ..."

"And even if we can't afford them," Laurie cut in, "Anthony and I still want to get married anyway ... besides, I don't really wear jewelry, and besides, these are modern times and rings are just an old fashioned formality ...."

"Laurie, dear," her mother interrupted, "perhaps we should talk about this later, that is, your father, you, and I ..."

"No rings? No rings? My God, how can you have a marriage without rings?" my mother gasped. "It's unheard of, it's sacrilegious! Antoni, Laurie, what're you thinking? Antoni, what kind of woman doesn't want a ring, ehh?"

"Momma, take it easy. I'm gonna take care of it, so stop worrying," I said, trying to keep the volume down.

"Maria," Laurie's father now spoke up, "aside from 'rings,' this is a, well, surprising development. What I mean to say is that we understood that our daughter and your son were ... what's the term?" he said, turning to his wife.

"Friends, George," Mrs. Burns replied, still smiling tightly.

"Yes, thank you ... friends. We had no idea that they were, uhh, what's that other term, dear?"

"Dating, Dad," Laurie finished, huffing and looking up at the ceiling.

"Oh, yes, dating ... a strange ritual ..." he said under his breath. "Frankly," he continued, "Gracie and I never expected it to become this ... serious. Laurie, we really need to speak of this at length and ..."

"Daddy, we have, remember?" Laurie replied, firmly. "Now Anthony and I are in love and we want to spend the rest of our lives together. Don't we?" she said, looking over at me.

"Yes, yes we do ... but look folks, if there's a problem we can always ..."

"Move the wedding up!" Laurie finished, giving me a piercing look as if to say: 'stand your ground.'

I swallowed hard. "Well, yes, perhaps a few weeks if need be," I winced, as Laurie ran her tongue across her mouth and looked away.

"Antoni!" my mother continued, again wagging a scolding finger, "you and this girl need to go and see the priest, he will know what to do."

"Ma, let's just take it slow and easy, alright?" I tried to reason.

"Slow and easy? You're telling us you want to get married in a few months and you want slow and easy? Antoni, this is July. Do you have any idea of how long it takes to plan a proper wedding? There's the invitations and the church schedule and the priest and the reception and notifying the relatives in Italy, plane flights and places for them to stay and the food for the reception and the orchestra and ..." my mother went on for at least five minutes until ...

"Stop!" Laurie announced and abruptly stood up. She drained her wine glass and took a deep breath. "Anthony and I have talked about eloping. This will save everyone the trouble and expense of a big, unnecessary, complicated wedding."

You could hear a pin drop in the room, especially after I stopped breathing. My mother just sat there with her mouth open, staring at Laurie. Then she closed her mouth, looked at me, stood up, spun around on her heal and stomped out of the room. A moment later we all jumped when we heard her bedroom door slam. I just sat there rubbing my forehead with my fingers.

"Well, would anyone like more wine?" Laurie said as cheerfully as she could muster, holding up her empty glass.

"Laurie, dear, perhaps we'd better go," her mother said.

"Yes, splendid idea, my dear," her father agreed, standing up.

“Oh now, Mom and Dad, let’s not be hasty, right, Anthony?” she said, looking over at me for support.

“Oh, yes, of course,” I fumbled, “she’ll get over it ...eventually. Look, she’s Italian, very emotional. I’m sure by tomorrow she’ll be fine ....”

“*No I won’t!*” Mother yelled from down the hall, then, the door slammed again, even harder this time.

Laurie poured herself more wine and sipped on it. I picked up the bottle and just drank.

“I’ll tell you what,” Mr. Burns said, “it’s getting late and I don’t feel like a train ride back to Long Island. Why don’t Gracie and I stay at a hotel this evening, and then tomorrow, after we’ve all had a good night’s rest, we can sort this whole matter out?”

I put the bottle down on the table. “That’s a fine idea, Mr. Burns,” I replied.

“Mom, Dad, you can stay with me,” Laurie said to them.

“Sweetheart, your apartment is very small and ...”

“I’ll sleep on the sofa, Mom. You and Daddy can take my bed,” she replied.

“Dear, you know how your father’s back is,” her mother emphasized, raising an eyebrow.

Laurie got the hidden message and nodded. “Oh yes, I forgot,” she answered, smiling courteously.

“Good, it’s settled then,” Mr. Burns said.

"Laurie, let me help clear the table," her mother offered.

"Oh no, that's fine, Mrs. Burns, I can do that," I quickly countered.

"It's alright, I got this" Laurie said, picking up some plates.

"Uh, Anthony, while the girls are doing that, why don't you and I get some fresh air?" Mr. Burns suggested.

"Fresh air, in New York?" I expressed humorously.

Laurie cleared her throat and shot me a look over her shoulder as she and her mother left the room carrying dirty dishes.

"Oh sure, Mr. Burns." I reacted accordingly.

I followed him out into the hall, down the stairs and out onto the street. Mr. Burns looked around and then turned to me.

"It's too bad the city lights obscure the night sky. Where we live it's nice to see the stars," he said.

"Well, I guess I'll have to come out there sometime," I replied.

Mr. Burns gave me a look I couldn't quite register at the time, but he smiled and invited me to walk with him.

"So, Anthony ... or do you prefer Tony?" he began.

“Oh well, most folks around the neighborhood just call me Anthony. Tony never really stuck,” I said.

“And you may call me George,” he said politely.

“Alright, George,” I repeated. “Hmm, George and Gracie ... Burns ... you know that’s interesting because I think there used to be an old radio program that featured a couple with that exact same name,” I said.

“Yes, I’m familiar with it,” George replied. “So Anthony, you’ve lived here in Brooklyn all of your life?”

“Yep, it’s my home.”

“I see. Laurie say’s you go to night school? What do you want to become?”

“Well, I’m taking computer courses to become a technician. I have a friend at the university where Laurie goes that said he’d get me a job there in the I.T. Department as soon as I pass.”

“I see. And that’s where you met Laurie?”

“Oh, yes sir. It was love at first sight. I was walking out one morning, after an interview, and she was walking in. She looked at me and *bam!* I guess I was smitten,” I said happily.

Mr. Burns looked up to the sky, closed his eyes, slowly shook his head and muttered something that sounded like ... “we warned her to be careful ....”

“Uh, excuse me, sir?” I asked.

George looked startled. “Oh, nothing, my boy, it’s nothing. So you began seeing each other right away then?”

“Well, yeah … we just started talking, had dinners together, I even sat in on a few of her classes and she came to night school with me a few times …. She’s real smart, I tell ya. I wish I had her brains. Anyway, one thing led to another and …”

“But, you haven’t copulated yet, obviously,” he said bluntly.

I stopped breathing for the second time that night as I looked over at him. He just looked straight ahead as we walked.

“Uhh, is that what she told you?”

“No, she doesn’t have to. I said it was obvious.”

“How’s that, sir?”

“Because you’re still alive.”

I guess I choked on some spit, or maybe it was the wine that was trying to crawl up my throat. Whatever the cause, I doubled over and hacked for dear life.

“Are you alright, Anthony?” George replied, putting a hand on my back.

I finally straightened up and gasped for breath. “Yeah, fine, sir,” I hiccupped through my tears as I blinked, trying to clear my vision … and then, just for a second, I thought I saw George change shape into something … I blinked some more and wiped my eyes with the backs of my hands. When I looked again, George was smiling sympathetically over at me and holding out a handkerchief.

"Are you sure you're alright, Anthony? Shall we get you some water?" he offered.

"No, no, I'm fine, Mr. Burns … I mean George," still blinking and trying to clear my head as I mopped my face with the cloth. "That was weird," I added.

"Weird?"

"Yeah, I mean, I thought I saw you … well, I must be seein' things, or it's the wine, or what you said a minute ago, or …" I babbled incoherently and then laughed, wishing I was someplace else.

George seemed to understand. "Sometimes tears act like a prism that distorts our vision … that, along with the alcohol, as you said. It's alright now, Anthony, I wouldn't worry. If you're up to it, let's continue our stroll," he said, patting my shoulder. I agreed, blew my nose real good and we continued walking.

"So, George, Laurie said you're an eye doctor?" I asked.

"Yes. Optometry is my specialty. Why, do you need glasses?"

"Uh, no. At least I don't think so."

"Well, that's good. Now, about what I said earlier …"

“Look, Mr., I mean, George, let me assure you that Laurie and I have never, I mean, we kiss and all that, but we haven’t ... I mean, I would never, because my mother would absolutely kill me and ...”

“Anthony, I believe you and I know my daughter would, hopefully, restrain herself.” George sighed. “She can be difficult to control at times. She has, shall we say, a lot of energy in her.”

“Yeah, I’ll say ... she kisses like a vampire on steroids.”

I don’t know what possessed me to say that out loud, but I caught my breath and looked over at George who simply sighed, nodded, and smiled in relative understanding.

“You know, Anthony, it wasn’t that many centuries ago that Gracie and I were young once and we were so passionate about each other that we could make liquid nitrogen boil for hundreds of miles in all directions,” he said, with a reminiscent look on his face.

I stared over at him, wide-eyed, and waited ... hoping for a punch line. He finally smiled, then chuckled. I joined him, reluctantly.

“Poetic license, my boy,” he added.

“Oh yeah, I get it,” I laughed politely. “Helps break the ice at parties, huh?”

“Yes, as you say,” he replied with a confused look on his face. “Now, Anthony, getting back to my daughter, I need to ask you how serious you are about this ... engagement?”

We both stopped near a small park. The street lights illuminated several couples walking hand in hand on the paved paths around and in between the trees and benches. I looked over at them and imagined myself walking with Laurie.

"Anthony?" I heard George's voice say.

"Oh, sorry. Look, Mr. Burns, I mean, George, Laurie and I *are* serious about getting married. Actually, she brought it up originally, that is, the subject. I just picked the right moment and capitalized on it."

"Laurie brought up the subject herself?"

"Uh, yes, sir. I thought she was kiddin' at first, but she said she was serious." Then I started to laugh. "She said if she ever met the right 'homo-sapien,' which I thought was a real hoot the way she put it, all 'scientific' and all, that she'd like to tie the knot. So, sometime later, that is, when I finally realized that I truly loved her, I proposed and she said yes."

George Burns looked dumbstruck and just stared at me for a few long minutes before he turned his back to me and looked up into the night sky again.

"Uhh, George, are you alright?" I finally said.

"Oh, yes, my boy, quite alright … it's just been a long day; perhaps we should make our way back now. I'm sure the girls are nearly done with the dishes and …"

Suddenly, from somewhere in the park, we heard a woman scream … and it was the kind of scream that made your spine turn to ice. I didn't hesitate. I just bolted towards the sound as the screaming continued.

"Anthony!" I heard George object from behind me, but I was already yards away from him on a dead run towards the center of the park where the woods were thickest. I heard the woman scream again and then I heard a man's rough voice. I broke through some bushes and took in the scene happening in a clearing intersected by a walking path. A hooded man had what looked like a female jogger down on the ground. I feared the worst so I yelled.

"Hey! Get off her!"

The man startled and looked up at me. He was wearing a ski-mask under the hood.

"Help me!" the woman begged.

The man jumped up and stood there, giving the woman the opportunity to struggle to her feet.

"Run!" I yelled to her. I didn't have to ask twice as she bolted down the path.

"You're dead," the hooded man said, and then I saw the gun. He pointed it at me … I didn't know what to do, I froze … I thought of Laurie, my mother … what the future might have been … and then, a split second later, the gunman screamed as if he were terrified, or on fire, or … and then he was gone … just gone, in a puff of vapor, like he was never there. I just stood frozen, my brain trying to figure out what I had just seen, but nothing registered. When I could unglue my feet, I walked over to where the thug had stood … there was nothing, nothing to suggest that he was ever there.

"Anthony," I heard a familiar voice say from behind me. I turned. It was George Burns standing there on the path. "We should get back; the girls will be worried if we're too late," he said calmly.

"Mr. Burns, George, did you see? I mean did you …"

"Come now, Anthony," he said, holding out a hand to me. I felt like a zombie as we walked out of the park and back onto the sidewalk. That's when I heard the sirens getting closer.

"She musta called the cops," I mumbled, then looked behind me.

"It's over now. Let's go home," George said, pulling gently on my arm.

After we had walked a little ways farther I asked. "George, what happened back there?"

"Why? Don't you remember? You frightened the criminal away and the young woman fled," George replied.

"No, no that's not what happened … the man, he, he just …"

"Just what?"

“Vaporized! My God, he just vanished, *poof*, into thin air,” I exclaimed loudly.

Several passersby looked curiously at us. George just smiled and waved at them.

“Yes, he was running rather fast,” George said.

I looked over at him with a serious look on my face. George smiled.

“Anthony, sometimes, under great stress, the mind plays tricks on us. It’s not unusual for our brains to …”

“He had a gun,” I said abruptly, “I saw it plainly. He said ‘you’re dead,’ I heard him. There was no reason for him to run, he had me cold,” I replied, my voice now shaking with emotion, and so were my knees.

George looked at me and sighed deeply, then he took my arm and we began to walk again.

“Anthony,” he said quietly, “Laurie loves you and I’m her father. That’s all that matters tonight.”

We didn’t talk anymore until we got to the apartment. Laurie and her mom were sitting out on the stoop waiting for us.

“Thought you guys might’ve gotten lost,” Laurie said.

“Did you two have a nice walk, dear?” Gracie asked.

“Yes, it’s a fine night for a stroll,” George replied.

I walked past them both up the stairs and inside.

"Anthony?" Laurie called, but I didn't wait. I went into our apartment, down the hall and stood before my mother's bedroom door, listening. Then I knocked lightly.

"Mom, you in there?"

"Not now, Antoni," she replied. "I'm not dressed and I have a headache. We'll talk tomorrow. Now let me sleep."

"Okay, momma, goodnight," I said. When I turned around, Laurie was standing in the hallway behind me. I stood there and looked at her and I guess my eyes told her everything, because she slid her hands into the front pockets of her jeans and looked down. She shook her head slowly and then looked up at me sorrowfully.

"Laurie," I managed to get out.

She shushed me with a finger over her lips and gestured for me to follow her to my room. Once we were inside she closed the door. I flipped on the lamp on the night stand.

"Where's?"

"They went to a hotel," she answered. "They said they'd see us tomorrow. Anthony, we need to talk. Dad told me about what happened in the park ..."

"I'll say we need to talk," I agreed, going over and sitting on my bed. "What's going on anyway? Is this some kinda T.V. show I'm on as a joke, huh?"

“No.”

“Well, sweetheart, it better be because I know what I saw and I’m telling ya, I’m not real clear on how I’m supposed to understand …”

“My father demolecularized that criminal to save your life. He did it for me,” she said simply. She just stood there and drew little circles with the toe of her sneaker.

“I’m sorry,” I replied, shaking the cobwebs out of my ears, “your father did what?”

“You heard me and you saw what happened.”

I jumped up. “What! What is he? What are you? Who are you?”

I guess I was getting a little loud because Laurie shushed me emphatically and came closer.

“Do you want your mother in here?” she whispered loudly.

I tried to back up, but the bed was in the way, so I sat down again.

“What are you?” I whispered back.

“Anthony, I’m your girlfriend, soon to be your wife, that’s who I am. And those two people who ate dinner with us tonight are my parents, George and Gracie … and my father saved your life tonight and he didn’t have to!” she fired as she leaned over in front of me and scolded as quietly as she could.

“Laurie, you haven’t answered my question yet.”

She straightened up and ran a hand through her long black hair. After sighing heavily she parked right next to me. The two of us just sat there, side by side, and said nothing for what seemed like a long time, then, she spoke.

"Alright, Anthony ... truth?" she asked.

"Oh, yeah," I replied in agreement.

She cleared her throat.

"My real name is Larrianthmatalliamathar."

I just looked at her, then, asked her to: "Say again ... slower."

She repeated it and then waited.

"Okay, keep going," I said, swallowing hard.

"My parents' names are not George and Gracie. And we're really not the Burns family from Long Island."

"No kidding," I blurted.

"Look, Anthony, just listen will ya?"

"Okay, I'm sorry."

"We do live on Long Island, well, at least for the time being."

More silence.

"Oh God, I hate to ask the next question," I lamented painfully.

Laurie's eyes began to fill up. "I love you, Anthony. I fell in love with you, I don't regret that. I want you to understand that before I go on."

"Okay, I believe you," I said.

"We're … tourists," she continued. "At least that's the word you would probably understand better. We came here to this planet to visit, well, my parents did. I was actually conceived here, that's why it's much easier for me to …" now she swallowed hard, "maintain my humanity."

"You're what?"

"My human form. My human form, Anthony."

She sounded frustrated.

"You're *not* human? Any of you?"

"No, sweetheart, we're not. Don't be dense. Could a human do what my dad did in that park?"

"Uh, no, I guess not. Could you do that?"

"Yeah and probably worse."

"Fer cryin' out loud, Laurie, or whatever your name is, you're gonna make me wet the bed here! By the way, *are* you a girl?" I blurted.

She slapped me across the shoulder, stood up and stomped to the other side of the room.

"*Ouch!* Take it easy, will ya?" I objected, grabbing my shoulder.

"Am I a girl ..." she repeated in a huff, crossing her arms and looking out the window.

I stood up. "Well, are you? Or are you some weird, spider looking, ten-eyed creature that ..."

She spun around ... and the next thing I knew I was plastered to my bedroom ceiling, unable to move.

"Ya know, I was warned about human men not maturing until they're what, a hundred and fifty? Oh, that's right, your species doesn't live that long, does it?" she said angrily.

"Uh, honey, I can't breathe," I managed to squeak out.

She closed her eyes and turned back around. I fell straight down, bouncing on my face, on the bed.

"My father warned me," I heard her say to herself.

I sat up, rubbing my neck. "Hey look, this is all new to me and rather sudden. So cut me some slack, will ya? And, the next time you levitate me like that, you can leave, okay?"

She turned back around and the water works started. I groaned and held an arm out to her. She ran over, sat next to me and buried her face in my neck.

"I'm sorry," she sobbed, "I just want a normal life, just like everyone else here on this world."

"A normal life? In Brooklyn?" I asked skeptically.

“Yes,” she said, sitting up and sniffing back her tears, “with you.”

“Is that possible? I mean you said that you’re not …”

“Human? No, I mean yes, I mean not yet … ohhh.”

“Look, just tell me what’s going on.”

“We, that is my parents and I, have an opportunity to go back to where we came from and rejoin our race. Dad’s tired of earth, say’s it stinks. But I wanna stay. The thing is, if I go back with them, I can never return here in this form, but, if I stay any longer, then I’ll stay this way permanently,” she said, touching herself.

“You mean you’ll be human?”

“Well yeah, kinda.”

“How do ya mean, ‘kinda?’”

“I mean I’ll look like this, and I’ll be mortal like the rest of you, but …”

“But what?”

She sighed and whipped her face. “My insides are different. My molecular structure is more dense.”

“Wait, are you saying you’ll be like superman … woman? Like what you just did to me or what your dad did in the park?”

“No, that will gradually disappear, thankfully. But, I will be strong and a few other things … look, Anthony, if you don’t want me, I’ll understand. I’ll go back with my parents when it's time."

"How soon?"

"Three months at the latest, but they want to leave early."

"How early?"

"This week. Look, Anthony, I wasn't going to say anything. I was just going to get married and let time do its work on me and everything would have been okay, but then tonight happened and …"

"Hey, I'm glad it happened," I said, stopping her. "A married couple can't have secrets from each other, especially one like this."

"So, what're you saying?"

"I'm saying, living here in Brooklyn all my life *is* like living around aliens, we're all from everywhere in this neighborhood. So, why not one from another planet?"

"Nebula actually," Laurie said, smiling thorough more tears.

"Nebula, Italy, Ireland, Russia, Manhattan, it's all the same when you come right down to it, isn't it?" I smiled back.

She laughed quietly and cried more. I got up and knelt down in front of her.

"Laurie Burns, or whoever you are, will you still marry me?" I asked. Then the water works really turned on.

"Yes, yes, Anthony Nicola Lazzaro, I will marry you.

"Good," I said, standing up, then pulling her up to me. We kissed and it still felt good.

"Now what?" she asked.

I looked at the clock. It was midnight. "Now we pretend like nothing happened in that park," I said.

"And you're okay with that now?"

"Yeah, I'll get over it. Hey, ya wanna go for a midnight stroll? I'll walk you home, how's that?"

"I'd like that," she said, taking my hand.

We left my room and tiptoed down the hall past my mother's room as she serenaded us with her snoring. We quietly closed the front door and skipped down the steps just in time to say hello to a passing beat cop. We started walking, arm in arm, down the sidewalk enjoying the balmy summer night. Tomorrow we would tell Laurie's parents our decision and square things with my mother. Laurie confessed that jewelry of any kind irritates her skin. She tried to explain the physics to me but I just held up my hand and told her not to worry about it. We walked and talked and planned our little future together right here in Brooklyn, on good old planet Earth ... and, you know, it worked out just fine.

Drone

Can any of us truly say that we are the sum total of ourselves? Or are we merely a reflection of something else or someone else, an echo of another reality, another life? How do we measure ourselves? By what ruler and who designed it? Who are we? Why are we? What is our purpose beyond the now? What is our name?

Unknown

I kept reading the words, over and over again, forbidden words, written a long time ago … or at least that's what I was told. I carefully folded the old, yellowed paper and slipped it back into my clothing unit. We are allowed to keep some personal effects but not many. They say personal items tend to distract the mind from the work assignments and they breed a mental disease called: Nostalgia. Most of us in our Pod just call it: 'The Longing.' They treat it with meds but the problem persists amongst our species. Sometimes, for advanced cases, it gets so bad, the pain that is, that we terminate our own lives or it's mercifully done for us. I understand this and accept it. It's better to go into 'the dark' rather than live with the pain.

The whistle beacon went off and it was time to go back to my assignment. I followed the line of others to my work station and slipped on another pair of the snug-fitting elastic gloves. The conveyor moved smoothly along in front of me carrying lines of circuitry boards to examine through the magnifier I had my face up against. If I saw a problem I would toss the board into a provided bin on the other side of the conveyor. Once the bin was full the contents were taken back to the labs for recycling.

The work period flew by, as it always does, and then the beacon sounded again. It was time to go back to our Pods for nourishment and rest. I stood in line and waited until we filed out onto a moving sidewalk that took us the rest of the way out of the factory. I stood behind another and stared blankly at the large number stenciled across the back of his clothing unit. We all looked straight ahead as we moved along as a group. Then there was an announcement.

"Drone designation 7667, report to Lab 14, Green Level."

That was me. I stepped off the walk and moved onto another going in the opposite direction. I made several of these transfers until I reached a lift. I stepped inside and said, "Green Level."

The doors silently slid closed behind me and the unit carried me straight up several floors, finally stopping at my destination. I disembarked and walked down a brightly lit white hallway, passing a number of closed doors with large numbers on the outside. I eventually arrived at Lab 14. I placed my hand on an identity panel on the wall. The door chimed and slid to the side. I entered and stood there waiting for further instructions.

"7667?" A white clad female Tech asked as she entered the room from an adjoining one.

"Yes," I replied.

"Come this way," she said briskly.

I followed her down another hall where we passed several, smaller rooms, containing others like myself, sitting naked on stainless steel examination tables. I felt a tightness growing in my chest but was reluctant to give evidence of distress. We stopped at the last room on the right.

“Go inside, remove your clothing, and then stand in front of the Disinfection Field. Make sure you do both sides for the full duration, you know the drill, and then sit on the table. A doctor will be with you shortly.”

“I understand,” I replied.

The Tech left. I entered and did what I was instructed. Afterward, I sat and waited on the bare metal table. As time passed, I was becoming hungrier and more uncomfortable. Also, the room temperature was not what I was accustomed to. My flesh started to pucker up in little humps. Then she walked in.

“Here we are,” she said pleasantly. She was another female, dressed in a long white lab coat and carrying a touch-pad. “My name is Doctor Worth and I’m here to give you an examination.”

“Excuse me, but I am not due for an E-val for another circadian cycle,” I said.

“Yes, I can see that on your chart,” she replied, checking her pad. “This is not a standard E-val, uhhh, 7667, but an examination for, let me see … other issues. Now, you’ll have to excuse me, I’m new here and I’m just a tad disorganized, please give me a moment and then we’ll get right at this,” she said, entering information on her pad.

“Please?” I responded.

She looked up. “Yes, what would you like?” she inquired.

“No, nothing … you said ‘please’ to me. Why?”

She looked confused. "Did I say something wrong?" she asked.

"No, of course not, it's nothing," I replied.

She smiled and went back to what she was doing. Then, apparently, something occurred to her. She turned, went over to a drawer under one of the counters and opened it. Not finding what she wanted at first she opened several more until she finally pulled out a white towel. Nodding in satisfaction she closed the drawer, returned and handed the towel to me.

"You may cover yourself with this," she said.

I unfolded the towel and looked at it. "This is too small for my entire body," I replied.

"Oh, no, no, it's to cover your ... you know your..." she pointed down to my groin and nodded.

I spread the towel over my lap and stared back at her. She smiled at me and then her face, for some unexplained reason, turned slightly red. I had never seen that before.

"Are you ill, Doctor?" I inquired.

"Me? No, oh no," she blushed, placing a hand on the side of her face. "Just the jitters I guess. By the way, are you cold?"

"Well, yes," I confessed.

She quickly went over and adjusted a wall unit and the room quickly became comfortable.

"There, how's that?"

“Adequate,” I said.

“Adequate, thank you,” she corrected, looking at me.

“I don’t understand your question,” I replied.

She held the touch-pad to her chest, came closer and leaned forward. “When someone does something nice for you, it’s proper to say ‘thank you.’”

I stared back at her in confusion. “What does ‘thank you’ mean and the other terms, ‘something nice’ and ‘the jitters’?”

She cleared her throat and stood up straight. She looked at me and sighed. “Never mind,” she said. “Let’s continue with the exam.”

After an hour or so had passed Doctor Worth had finished with the examination.

“You may get dressed now, 7667,” she said, as she busily imputed information into her touch-pad.

“Very well, Doctor. May I be permitted to inquire if you have found any abnormalities?”

She stopped typing and looked up. “Well, of course you can. Now, your bios all seem to be within normal parameters ... let me see,” she muttered to herself, as she touched her screen, “you were generated in 2038 and you are twenty-five cycles in age, male, no genetic aberrations, intelligence is, hmm, above average for a drone ... hmm, now that’s unusual according to my grid ... let’s see here ...” she ran her fingers around her screen to access more data. “It’s also odd that they’ve decided to keep you on the factory floor. I wonder if there's a glitch in the programming. I'll make a note of this and perhaps we can get you transferred to a better …"

"That won't be necessary, Doctor Worth," I interrupted.

"I don't understand," she replied.

"As you said initially, you're new here. It would be better for me if I stay at my current work assignment."

She lowered her touch-pad and looked at me. "Well, it's my understanding that you will be assigned to where your analysis places you, and based on this, you should be at a much higher level of …"

"I am a drone, Doctor. A laboratory contrived product for use in the labor force. I only wish to complete my cycles with as little attention as possible."

"I'm sorry, I don't understand," she replied.

I stood up and the towel fell to the floor. "This is the first analysis where the results have come back indicating that my intelligence has risen beyond normal parameters for a drone. Check and see how much since my last examination."

She ran her fingers quickly over the screen and looked. "Thirty percent," she replied, "your stats indicate that your intelligence has risen thirty percent since your last analysis. Why is that?"

"I don't know," I replied soberly. "But what I do know is when this has happened to others in my Pod they have been transferred out of the factory."

"Well, that's a good thing, isn't it?"

"No. They were never seen again. We found out later that they were most likely recycled."

"What? No. No you must be mistaken, 7667. There are rules that prevent ..."

"Doctor, you apparently are not only new, but naive as well. It is none of my business but where do you come from?"

"The Mid-West, Illinois. After I got my Ph.D. I spent some time on the Space Station and then I was assigned here."

"So then you are not familiar with drone culture?"

"Well, I took a class on it and I was briefed before I arrived at this plex, I mean facility."

I laughed at her even though it was against the rules. It had been the first time I had done so in a very long time and it felt strange. She seemed confused by my outburst.

"I didn't think you folks were capable of ..."

"Laughter?" I finished for her. "Yes, we have the capabilities to do a great many things; we just do not have the occasion or are permitted to."

"I'm sorry for that. And I'm sorry you think that I'm naïve. I probably am."

"You should not feel sorry," I replied.

"But I am naïve. Tell you what, why don't you enlighten me? But first, would you please get dressed," she said, clearing her throat and pointing to my coveralls hanging on a hook.

I did so. Meanwhile, Doctor Worth found a chair and brought it over to me, and then she went and retrieved another from across the hall and brought it into the room. She invited me to sit. She began to do the same, but then stopped.

"Oh, I'll be right back. Stay put," she said.

"Yes, Doctor," I replied obediently.

She returned a few minutes later with a tray carrying two hot meal PACs, along with utensils and beverages. She placed the tray on the examination table and took one of the PACs and beverages for herself. She sat down across from me and slid open the PAC. The room immediately became filled with the rich aroma of baked chicken and dumplings.

"This is my favorite," she said. "I got you the same. Go ahead and eat."

"Doctor, we are not permitted to eat with ..."

"I give permission; now eat," she interrupted.

I opened my PAC and beverage container and dug in.

"This is not what we are normally allowed to eat," I said as I chewed. "This type of nutrition is usually only for ... humans."

She started choking for some reason. “Doctor, are you alright?” I asked. She nodded as she swigged down some of her beverage.

“I’m fine, just took too big a bite I guess … you said this food is only for who?”

“Humans,” I replied, without looking up.

“You mean people like me?”

“Yes.”

“So, what’re you?”

I stopped eating and looked at her. “I’m a drone.”

“But, you’re also human and …”

“No!” I replied emphatically. “And you should know better than to say such things to me. Humans are born from other humans. Drones are grown in a crèche and distributed where needed by the State. You should know this.”

“I do know this,” she replied, putting her fork down. “I just …” something caught in her throat, “I just don’t believe in it. That’s not how I was raised.”

“Raised?”

“Yes, brought up by my parents on our farm in Illinois. There were no drones where I lived, just livestock … farm animals to take care of and nurture. I probably should’ve been a veterinarian, but I chose medicine.”

“Why?”

"Because I enjoy helping people."

"Then why are you here with me?"

"Because I want to help you."

"Why? I am not a person. You should have become a veterinarian, they work with animals ... like us, like me," I said, touching my chest.

We both finished eating our food in silence. Then she took our empty PACs and shoved them down the waste disposal unit.

"Shall I leave now and return to my Pod?" I asked.

"No ... I mean, would you mind staying a bit longer? I want to do some personal research and I have many questions. Will you stay?"

"If it is your wish, Doctor," I replied. "My sleep period doesn't begin for several more hours."

"Good. Thank you," she said, picking up her touch-pad and entering information.

"You are welcome, Doctor," I replied uncomfortably.

She looked up, smiled warmly at me, and then returned to her typing. After a few minutes she spoke.

"Now, 7667 ... oh, wait, this will never do. You need a proper name."

She paused and ran her eyes across the ceiling. "Let me see, what would be a good, manly name for you, any ideas?"

“My designation is 7667, why would I require another?”

“No, you don’t understand. A name is not a designation or a label, it identifies you as an individual. It’s personal; it’s who you are to others.”

I gave her a confused look.

“It’s like my name,” she said.

“You are Doctor Worth,” I replied.

“Yes, but my first name is Ruth. My full name is Ruth Worth. That’s who I am, an individual.”

“I have no such title,” I replied.

“And that’s why I want to give you one.”

“Why?”

“Because I want you to see that you are an individual, not just an assignment ... not just a drone.”

“But I am a drone.”

She held up a single digit. “Not today. Now let’s pick you a proper name.”

We both sat thinking ...well she did. After a few more minutes her eyes seemed to light up.

“You know, you remind me of someone I knew in high school, a real nice guy. His name was Simon, the last name doesn’t matter. So, what do you think of Simon?”

“I do not know him.”

“No, I mean Simon for your name. How would you like to be called Simon?”

I sat there and simply couldn’t think for a few moments. Then, I felt an unusual, warm, pleasant, feeling sweep over me. I found myself smiling again causing the muscles in my face to ache.

“I take that as a yes?” she asked.

“Yes,” I replied, “but, I’m not sure it is permitted outside of this room.”

“Well then, we’ll just have to make it our little secret, won’t we?” she smiled.

“Deception is forbidden for a drone.”

“That’s alright; I give you permission to keep this just between us. So, as long as we’re together, you are Simon and I’m Ruth. Are we agreed?”

My smile vanished and I felt uncomfortable.

“Simon, are we agreed?”

I thought about what she was asking, and then I remembered what I read earlier on the paper that was in the pocket of my clothing unit. I put my right hand to my chest and felt the folded document. I took several breaths and then I said: “Yes, we are agreed … Ruth.”

And so it began. She would ask questions and I would answer. Questions about how I began, my training, my Pod mates, my work assignments… everything she could think of to ask about the existence of a drone. Finally she yawned and put down her touch-pad.

"Thank you, Simon, that was very enlightening. I had no idea. I'm ... sorry," she said.

"Sorry? For what?"

"For you. For you and the others of your kind. You simply exist. You're like slaves in this society. I disagree with what's happening on moral grounds."

"Moral grounds?"

"Yes, the principals of basic right and wrong. Good and evil."

"Ruth, drones are neither good nor evil. We simply serve a function. We are made to carry out our functions and live out our cycles for the greater good."

"Who's greater good, Simon? Who benefits?"

"Why, your kind naturally ... and us, we are provided for adequately."

"But you're not free. Free to choose, free to go where you want, free to make your own choices, don't you see?"

"I understand your concern and ..." I hesitated.

"And what?"

"I will admit that I have had aberrant thoughts from time to time ... thoughts about my purpose, even my existence, as have others. We are required to report these, but ..."

"But?"

"I haven't yet. I usually ignore them and they go away."

"Why?"

"Because it simply isn't our function to adjust our …"

"Programming? Isn't that what you wanted to say?"

"No. We use the term 'cultivation;' it makes us who we are."

"Drones."

"Yes, that is my function."

"Simon, don't you see, that makes you nothing more than a biological robot."

"I am not a machine, a robot. I am more."

"How?"

"I can reason in the abstract. Take the initiative to solve complex situations, display loyalty to a purpose and to my Pod mates …"

"Can you fall in love?"

"Love?" I replied, "I have heard about such emotions. How does that contribute to my function?"

She sighed heavily and chuckled. "Well then, Simon, you're just a very fancy machine, grown in a Petri dish to serve a mindless function, and then be recycled … hmm, some life."

"What do you suggest as an alternative? Shall we go back to robotics? History teaches us that did not work, millions died."

"Yes, I remember my history, and, no, I have no desire to return to that. But this isn't any better. In fact in some ways it's worse."

"How so?"

"It's worse because drones are sentient. You have a will, but it's not free. You have been biologically programmed to function like a machine. You are not free."

"Ruth, may I ask you a personal question?"

"Of course."

"Are you an abolitionist?"

She sat there and worked her jaw for a few moments before answering.

"And if I am?"

"Then you would be considered an enemy of the State. Do you realize that?"

"Yes, I do. However, I am not part of that movement."

"You mean not at present?"

She stood up, went to the counter, drew herself a container of water and drank it down.

"Would you like some?" she asked.

"No."

She then returned to her seat. "Simon, I will admit that I have read some of their literature. The fact is they are very active where I'm from. They hope, someday, to have legislation passed to make drones citizens with full rights and freedoms. I look forward to seeing that happen. Don't you?"

Now it was my turn to stand up and walk around. I thought about what she said ... and it made me nervous.

"You're afraid of that possibility, aren't you, Simon?"

I turned and looked at her. "Your words make me feel strangely," I confessed. "I cannot imagine life outside my function, my Pod. I, we, would all be lost ...."

"Perhaps at first, but I think eventually, once you got a real taste of freedom, human freedom, you would like it."

"Human freedom is for humans."

"Simon, you *are* human, in every way. You and the others have just been convinced that you are not. You've been indoctrinated that you are sub-human, that you can't be changed, but you can. You can be retrained. It would be just like learning a new function, but you have to want it. You have to want to be free."

I looked at the interval measuring unit on the wall.

"Ruth, it is time for me to enter my sleep cycle. I must leave now."

She stood up. "Very well, I have all the data I need for now," she said. "Would you be willing to return and continue our discussion?"

"That would be viewed as suspicious as my examination is now completed."

"Not necessarily. Sometime data can be lost ... and I'm new here, remember?" she smiled.

"I understand. You plan on using deception, yes?"

She just smiled. "Now, in the meantime, I want you to swallow two of these a day, one right after your sleep cycle and one before, understand?" she said, handing me a small plastic-wrapped unit containing several small blue pills.

"Am I ill, Doctor?"

"Keep these out of sight and someplace safe. You will be summoned."

"I understand."

"Thank you, Simon."

"I've done nothing to require your thanks."

"Oh, but you have. Now, you should leave, 7667."

She turned and accessed a control that opened the room door. Then she looked at me, smiled, and nodded. I quickly left the room and the facility. I went to the nearest turbo I could find to transport me to my Pod location. As I sat and rode, I felt uncomfortable, my head buzzing with thoughts that I was not used to having ... forbidden thoughts. When I arrived at my destination, I went to my quarters, imbibed one of the pills she had given me, and lay on my sleeping frame. Before I realized it, my sleep cycle was over and I was, again, back in line going to my work station at the factory. We all took turns, like we always have, placing our palms on one of the Bio-Security Panels in the check-in kiosk, as an automated voice would announce our designation.

"7667 to station four ... next ..."

This never bothered me before, why should it? But, on this work cycle, it did. I walked away from the machine saying to myself, "My name is Simon."

Several work and sleep cycles passed, and then, again, there was an announcement.

"Drone designation 7667 report to Lab 14, Green Level."

"I smiled to myself and my heart raced as I moved to the conveyance that would take me to the lifts to the upper floors. When I arrived at Lab 14, I was, again, instructed to remove my clothing and disinfect. I complied and waited. Finally, she entered the room. After making sure the door was secure, she smiled and said, "Hello again, Simon ... you may get dressed now."

I did so, and we sat down together. She talked about wonderful possibilities for the future of drones everywhere ... and then especially for me.

"Why am I so special?" I asked.

"Because you have very active brain functions and your intellect is above average. I'm trying to hide these indicators from my superiors so that we can continue with our discussions. Simon, if they discover these so called abnormalities in you they could ..."

"Move me to a better position? You know better than that now, don't you, Doctor?"

"Yes, thanks to you I'm no longer naive."

"It's just a matter of time then before I am discovered," I said.

She seemed to be distressed by this fact. "Yes, and I've been thinking a lot about this over the past few days," she said, looking at me, "Simon, would you be willing to escape?"

"Escape? Do you mean leave without authorization? Leave my Pod, my assignment?" I replied in surprise. "This is not permitted. That action would result in ..."

"Termination," she finished for me. "Yes, I know. I've made the inquiries, but what's the alternative? If they find out the results of your exams then what? You said it yourself earlier, others were transferred ..."

"No, not transferred, recycled," I said, standing up. I looked down at my hands and they were shaking. I also felt an urgent need to relieve myself of water. I requested to use the facility in the room. Ruth pointed to a door. When I returned she also seemed in a state of agitation on my behalf.

"Simon, we have to get you out of here, out of the complex and far away."

"I do not have the proper authorization and travel codes that would allow me to ..."

"I can get them for you," Ruth said, coming over and taking my arm. "I'll help you get away," she said almost in a whisper.

"Away? To where? Where would I go?"

"There are places, secret places, far away from the cities that others, others like you, can go and live. Simon, you can live free! Think of it."

"I have thought of it, but I am unsure."

"I know how you feel. I know what it's like to be afraid, but I can help you if you let me."

"You've done this before, Ruth?"

"Yes."

'For other drones?"

"Yes. On other assignment at another Plex ... for a female."

"And this female is safe?"

"Yes, safe and happy in her new home far away

from the Plexes, the Factories, the Pods."

"Did this female have a name?"

Ruth smiled. "Yes, we settled on Rose."

"Can I meet her?"

"If you end up in the same district she is in, yes."

"I don't understand?"

"Simon, there's not just one place to hide. This is a big continent and we try to find the safest escape route to the safest location for you. Sometimes it's near, other times it's far away, it depends. What matters is the sentinels won't find you. In fact, if we do this right, the State will never bother you again."

"How is that possible?"

"Because they'll think you're dead,"

"You mean recycled?"

"Yes, that's why I'm here, along with a few others who work in this complex. We can change the system input files, your files. Make it show that you were recycled."

I ran my fingers through my hair as my mind raced with indecision. Ruth observed my distress and held my shoulders.

"Simon, you can do this, but it has to be what you want, I won't force you, but it has to be accomplished soon."

“Why?”

“Because I think I’m being watched.”

“Watched? Ruth, we are all watched.”

“I know, but this is different. I’m being evaluated every day, which means I could be transferred anytime, like I was to here from my last assignment.” She turned and folded her arms. “Simon, there was another drone I was helping at another Plex but there wasn’t enough time for me to get him away before I was reassigned ... he didn’t make it.”

“He returned to his Pod?”

Ruth looked away momentarily and rubbed the back of her neck. “He couldn’t integrate back into his function ... he became unstable and ...”

“I understand. This happens sometimes to us. I am aware of it, but we never speak of it openly in the Pod. We are warned about our thoughts, thoughts about possible existence beyond our function, about what we have been talking about.”

“So, someone has approached you before?”

“No, never ... it’s just ...” I reached into my inside pocket and took out the folded piece of paper and handed it to her. Ruth carefully opened it and read.

“Simon, do you know who wrote this?”

“No. No one knows, but I was told that the words are very old.”

“Yes, they go back to the beginning of the drone program in the 2020’s. Did you know that a drone wrote this?”

“Drones don’t write.”

“Well, this one could and did. He tried to start a movement to give drones some rights, but they prevented him and he disappeared.”

“Where?”

“No one knows, but some of his writings still survive, like this one,” she said, handing the paper back to me. “Don’t get caught with that,” she warned.

I smiled at her. “I will not.”

“Simon, there’s real hope for you now that I’ve seen that paper.”

“Perhaps so. Perhaps it’s time to put my fear aside,” I said looking at her.

Ruth smiled at me and came closer. “Good. If that’s the case then we need to start moving on this immediately, but we can’t run the risk meeting like this for another false examination, they will certainly become suspicious. So ...” she quickly looked at her time unit attached to her wrist, “I need to contact my support and see if we can move you tonight. Are you willing to leave tonight?”

I started to breathe heavily. “Yes, I will go when you say.”

"Good. Now, you wait here while I go and try to set this up. In the meantime, try to relax. If another Tech comes in, tell them I had to step out and that I will be returning to finish the exam, understand?"

"Yes."

"Good," Ruth said as she turned and cycled the door to open. "I'll be right back" she said, and then she left, left me alone with my thoughts.

I tried to sit on the table but my skin felt as if it were crawling. So I walked around the office poking my head into drawers and cabinets to keep myself busy, even though I knew it wasn't permitted. Then, after some time had passed, another white clad female Tech walked in.

"7667?" she asked.

"Yes," I responded.

"You are to come with me."

"The Doctor said she would return to finish my ..."

"Doctor Worth has been detained with another assignment. Your examination will be administered by another doctor. Come with me now," she insisted.

I followed her out of the room, down the hall and into another examination room.

"Remove your clothing and sit on the table," I was told and then the Tech left. I did what I was told and sat naked on the table. I was now experiencing a sense of foreboding as I sat there shivering. Finally, a man wearing a long lab coat came in and he wasn't alone, he had another man with him, wearing a uniform and a helmet. I recognized him as a Security Enforcer.

"Now, let me see, you are drone 7667, correct?" the man in the lab coat asked.

I wanted to say my name was Simon, but I restrained myself and simply answered, "Yes."

"And this is your second E-val, is this correct?"

"Yes."

"And why is that do you suppose?"

"I was informed that the data of the first E-val was accidently lost or corrupted."

"And who informed you of this?"

"Doctor Worth."

"She gave you her name?"

"It was displayed on her Identity Badge as is yours, Doctor Stewart."

The doctor looked irritated for a moment, but then cleared his throat.

"I see. Did Doctor Worth say anything else to you?"

"Such as?"

"Anything else that we should know about?"

“No.”

“And you’re telling me the truth?”

“Sir, I am a drone, what else would I tell you?”

The doctor looked over at the guard who remained expressionless, then back at me.

“Very well, we will proceed with the exam.”

And he proceeded, but not as kindly as Doctor Ruth had. Later, as I dressed, Doctor Stewart was busily entering date into his touch-pad. At one point, he stopped and showed the guard a particular screen. The guard nodded to him and then looked at me. I turned my back to them both as I fastened my collar. There was a reflective panel on the wall in front of me so I was able to observe the goings on behind me. The guard touched a communication unit on his helmet and quietly spoke into his mouth piece. Then the doctor quickly left.

I turned around and looked at the guard.

“Sir, if I am finished I will return to my Pod,” I said.

“You just wait right here,” he replied, pointing a finger at me.

“Is there a problem?” I inquired.

“Not for long,” the guard said.

“May I ask if Doctor Worth will be joining us?”

The guards jaw tightened. “Well now, what’s that to you lab-rat, huh?”

“I was just curious, sir.”

“Oh yeah, since when are drones curious about anything?” he said, stepping closer to me.

“Only in that she said she would return, nothing more.”

“Well, for your information, not that it’s any of your business, Doctor Worth has been detained for questioning.”

“I see. She seemed adequately qualified in the performance of her assignment.”

“You’re pretty chatty for a meat-stick, aren’t ya?”

“I mean no disrespect.”

“Well, I suppose it doesn’t matter if I tell you anything,” he snickered, “seein’ as how you’re gonna be transferred to a new assignment real soon.”

“I see. Will I be able to return to my Pod?”

The guard laughed out loud. “Not where you’re goin’ lab-rat.”

“And the Doctor?”

“We’ve been watching her ever since she transferred into this Plex, and right now she’s in big trouble. That’s all I’m gonna say to ya. Now you just be a good boy and wait ....”

The security guard continued to talk, but I couldn’t hear him as little explosions kept going off inside me. I felt an emotion I had never felt before in my entire existence. I believe it is called anger. It had been rumored in my Pod community that we were given additives in our food and water that suppressed anger and other volatile emotions, but we never paid much attention to such rumors, it was not part of our function. Now, however, I felt differently, as I balled my right fist.

"Hey, toad, you hearin' me?" the guard sneered, poking me in the shoulder.

"Yes, I hear you. Where is she?" I said evenly.

"What?"

"Where's Doctor Worth? Where is she being held?"

"Well, you're a nosey little test-tube mistake, aren't ya?"

I didn't realize I had hit him until after he was sliding down the opposite wall of the examination room. I must admit it felt good and my head was clear as to my purpose. He groaned and started to access his communications device. I quickly went over and yanked off his helmet. Then, I grabbed him under his chin and lifted him off the floor. I was told once when I was young, by an older member of my Pod group, that most drones are inherently strong. The reason for this was that we were genetically engineered that way in order to accomplish the most arduous tasks assigned to us. I guess he was right as I seemed to be exerting very little effort in handling the guard. He coughed and sputtered as he hung on to my wrists with both hands.

"You will tell me where she is being held or I will separate your head from your spinal column, do you understand?" I said to him.

"Yeah, yeah ..." he croaked. "Down two levels, administration wing, detention section one ... what're you anyway?"

"I am *not* a what, I am a who ...and my name is Simon," I replied, as I squeezed harder, forcing him into unconsciousness.

I laid him on the floor and stood up. Then I measured him with my eyes and discovered that we were close to the same physical size. I laid him on the exam table, stripped him naked, and put on his uniform and helmet. I could hear the background chatter in the helmet's speakers. Other guards were reporting in. Then, I heard someone say they were escorting a woman detainee from the detention center to the Heliport for transport. I put the helmet visor down and walked out of the room. I passed several Techs who paid no attention to me as I entered a tube going down. When I had reached the desired level, I walked out to face more staff who quickly lowered their eyes and walked past me. I started walking, not really knowing where I was going, when a female exited into the hall in front of me from another room.

"You there," I said gruffly, "where is the quickest way to the Heliport from this floor?"

The woman seemed shaken by my stopping her, but she gave me directions. I walked away, rounded the corner and then broke into a dead run to the end of the hall and through a set of doors with stairs leading down several levels where I was deposited into a parking garage lined with a variety of human conveyance vehicles. I shoved the visor up to see more clearly as I walked quickly around the cavernous garage. Then I saw several people exit from another door farther away, two men, Sentinels and between them was ...

I bolted for them, running as fast and as quietly as I could. The Sentinels had hold of each of her arms as they marched towards the back of the garage where the Heliport pad was located outside. I came up behind them, grabbed each guards' neck just below the rim of their helmets and squeezed. They grunted and dropped to the floor. Then I turned to their prisoner ... it wasn't Ruth. The young woman looked startled.

"Don't be afraid," I said, "I'm looking for Doctor Ruth Worth."

"She's already in the transport ship outside. They're taking us to an interrogation center outside the Plex, can you help us?"

"Yes, show me."

I dragged the two guards out of sight and then the young woman and I ran for a far exit leading out of the garage. Once we got there, we carefully opened the door a crack. I could see a waiting ship with an open side-hatch idling on the landing pad with one guard standing near it. I turned to the woman.

"What is your name?"

"Addison … Beverly."

"Addison Beverly, you are my prisoner, understand?"

"Yes."

I took her arm as we both walked outside and marched towards the ship. When I was near enough to the guard I announced …

"I have the prisoner Addison Beverly to be transported to the Interrogation Center along with the prisoner Ruth Worth."

"You alone?" the guard asked.

"Yes."

"There should be two of you, where's the other guard, what happened?"

"The other didn't show up. I was told to bring this woman here at once."

"Oh yeah, by whom? This ain't regulation … lemme check on this," he replied, accessing his COM.

"That won't be necessary," I said.

"Oh yeah, why not?"

I grabbed him by the font of his tunic, lifted him over my head and then slammed him into the side of the ship. He went limp, but was breathing.

"Inside!" I said to the woman.

She scurried in and I was right behind her. Once

inside, I saw Ruth strapped into a seat with a guard sitting across from her.

"About time you got here," the unsuspecting guard said to me, "we're behind schedule … and what was that banging outside?"

"I don't know," I replied, and then I hit him in the face.

I raised my visor and looked over at Ruth.

"Simon!" she exclaimed.

"How many more?" I asked.

"Just the pilot," she said.

"Where do you want to go?" I asked.

"Tell him to fly us outside the Plex, go south; don't let him talk to anyone on the COM-Link."

"I understand," I said. I pulled the unconscious guard out of his seat and threw him outside. Then, after closing the hatch door, I went into the pilot's cabin.

"Hey, what's goin' on back there?" he said as I entered and sat down into the co-pilot's seat.

"Lift off, exit the Plex and go south." I said.

"Huh? That's not our flight plan," he objected.

I reached over and changed his mind. I removed his helmet and COM-Link, then ordered him to lift off, and we did, straight up and then due-south for a long time.

After a while, Ruth came in and gave instructions on a particular location that she called 'co-ordinance.' The pilot seemed to understand, but I kept a hand on his shoulder just in case. We finally landed in pitch darkness and Ruth told the pilot to 'kill the landing lights.' She then told him to adjust his COM to a certain frequency and make contact with whomever replied. He reluctantly did so. After several tries, contact was made and Ruth spoke to whoever it was. A short time later several land traveling vehicles arrived with men in them. They seemed happy to see Ruth and the Beverly woman. The pilot was detained, while the rest of us drove away and rode most of the rest of my sleep cycle until the sun came up. I found myself in a wide, strange and wonderful place. The land seemed to pile up high into the sky, while in other places we traveled through, it stretched out, hot and barren in all directions with unusual plant life haphazardly growing all around. We stopped and got out once to rid ourselves of water. I tried to touch one of the strange plants, but it stung me with a spike.

Ruth laughed and told me to be careful. After cleaning the wound, she took my finger and put it into her mouth. It felt better immediately, but it made me feel ... unusual inside my chest. We drove more until we came to a small settlement with dozens of other people. Ruth said they used to be like me. They welcomed us and made me feel safe.

Since my arrival here in my new desert home, I've met many former drones and I call them by their names now ... Joe, Sam, Betty, Sarah, Rose and others. After a while, Ruth no longer has to give me pills to wean my body off the drugs I had been given most of my existence back in the Pod. Now my head is clear and I'm learning to have real purpose ... and a life. Also, I'm finding that things aren't as strange as they once were ... well, except for one new custom that I'm still getting used to ... Ruth often presses her lips against mine. She says that eventually I'll figure it all out. I hope so. It makes me smile.

17862489R00162

Made in the USA
Charleston, SC
04 March 2013